black
flowers

black flowers

jesse muchmore

DARK
CURRENTS
PRESS

Dark Currents Press
Clearwater, Florida

Copyright © 2019 Jesse Muchmore

Cover design by Vince Haig
Interior design by Euan Monaghan
Edited by Daniel Johnson
Copyedited and proofread by Stephanie Cohen

Printed in the United States of America.
ISBN: 978-1-7338947-0-8 (Paperback)
ISBN: 978-1-7338947-1-5 (eBook)

Library of Congress Control Number: 2019904211

www.jessemuchmore.com

To Jenn, for always believing in me.

To all of the friends
who have read my work over the years
and encouraged me to keep writing.

"And Jacob wrestled with the angel …"

Hosea 12:4

CONTENTS

THE RIVER

Come down to the river
and clean your hands
The water will wash away
all your sins

I know, I know
what that awful man made you do
But now he no longer
has a hold on you
And desperate times,
they call for desperate measures
But now your crimes,
they've made you question
who you are

So come down to the river
and clean your hands
The water will wash away
all your sins

I know, I know
this is not what you wanted
Goes to show
Just how cruel this life can be
Now let those tears roll on down your face
It's not your fault
You did not choose this disgrace

I know, I know
what that awful man made you do
But now he no longer
has a hold on you
And desperate times,
They call for desperate measures
But now your crimes,
they've made you question
who you are

So come down to the river
and clean your hands
The water will wash away
all your sins

THE EVIL AMONG US

Jim swung the bat with as much force as he could, but Raymond's curveball had improved.

"Strike three! You're outta there, Oreo!" Stevie yelled from the sidelines.

"All right, all right. You don't have to rub it in," Jim said, dropping the bat and returning to the area they had designated as the outfield.

Over the past few weeks this was the five boys' afternoon ritual. As soon as they got home from school, they would meet up in the vacant lot behind the housing complex in which they all lived and play ball until the sun went down. They all dreamed of being ballplayers ever since they'd seen Willie Mays' performance in the World Series the year before. Mays' unbelievable over-the-shoulder running catch of Vic Wertz's long drive was all any sports fan could talk about for weeks.

He was now their collective idol, though the other boys always told Jim he could only hope to ever be half as good as Mays since he was only half black. As an eleven-year-old biracial boy, Jim was always caught between two worlds, never feeling that he fully belonged in either. Life had only become harder now that the southern school system of Arish, Tennessee was forced to integrate by the federal government. Racial tensions ran high, and Jim never knew which side was going to strike at him first. In fact, the only reason he was tolerated among this group of young, black boys was because of his best friend Raymond, but they were quick to let Jim know his true place as soon as Raymond was out of earshot. He seemed to be the only one that wasn't bothered by Jim's background.

"Raymond! Dinner time!" Raymond's father's voice carried from the window of their third floor apartment.

"Damn, guess we'll have to call it a draw, boys," said Raymond.

"Even though we probably would've beat 'em." Jim shot a grin to Raymond.

"You wish, half-breed!" Edmund sneered. The boys gathered up their bats and made their way back inside. Jim knocked before entering the front door to their apartment, just as his mother had instructed him to do. She stuck her head out from the bathroom as he proceeded down the hallway to his room and said, "It's just me here."

Jim knew the eyeshadow and dark red lipstick on her face meant she would be bringing a man home tonight. After dropping his catcher's glove on his bed, he returned to the bathroom doorway and watched his mom pin up her bright red hair. She glanced at him, taking note of the disappointed look on his face, and said, "Don't look at me like that. You know I have to get at least a few customers a week or we don't eat. Plus, a lot of guys don't like coming into this neighborhood so I might not even have to bring him here, and you're usually asleep by then, anyways."

He knew she was right, but he also knew this meant he'd be making his own dinner tonight and tucking himself in. He watched as his mother attached her stockings to the small white girdle around her waist and thought to himself how lovely she was. Her soft, white skin and gentle demeanor contradicted the hardships she endured as a single mother and the sole provider for their household. There was a nurturing way about her that served as a stark contrast to the world. He knew this was the same reason that she was always able to attract male customers without difficulty.

She wiggled into a form-fitting red dress and had Jim zip up the back for her. Then she turned to him and held his face in her hands. "You know I love you, honey, and I wouldn't do this if I didn't have to." She kissed his cheek, leaving a trace of lipstick, and then she was out the door.

He spent a few hours attempting to do homework, but quickly found that any and everything was able to distract him from it, so he went into the living room and turned on the radio. He listened to President Eisenhower make a speech about the Treaty for Open Skies but quickly grew bored and settled instead on a rock station playing the "latest and greatest" hits by Chuck Berry, Bill Haley and the Comets, and others. He wished he had a television like many of the white kids at school, but as far as he knew no one in his complex owned one. Then again, this was public housing meant for poor blacks.

After a dinner of thin, meatless marinara sauce and spaghetti noodles, he opted for a quick bath and got in bed a little earlier than usual. It had been a long day and he was worn out from the competitive ball game with Raymond and the other boys. He began to wonder how exciting and different the lives of the rich and famous must be. He imagined himself as a famous baseball player traveling around the world and taking his mom out to dine in fancy restaurants every night. He drifted off to sleep with a smile on his face.

"I'm fine, I'm fine," Ella said with a slur in her voice that indicated she was quite the contrary as Winston helped her into his car.

"Whatever you say, Ella," said Winston as he crawled into the driver's side.

She'd had a few drinks, which was quite unusual for her, especially when she was working, but Winston had insisted. Since he was one of her regular customers, she allowed herself to let down her guard a little and relax. They both knew he'd be coming home with her by the end of the night, regardless.

"We better get you home quickly if I'm going to get my money's worth," he said with a playful smile.

Ella smiled and rested her head against the leather seat. *Winston's a nice guy, even if he is into some weird sexual stuff,* she thought. His typical request was for her to speak to him like a little girl and refer to him only as "daddy" when they were in bed together. She'd done far kinkier things for customers, so she was happy to indulge his fantasies if it kept him coming back.

After parking the car on a side street the two of them made their way up the stairs. Ella made sure to keep one hand on the railing and the other firmly wrapped around Winston's arm when she began to realize the alcohol was indeed affecting her sense of balance. They made it to her door and Ella removed her key from her purse and then paused. She stared at Winston for a moment then held a finger up to her lips and whispered, "My son's asleep, so I'd appreciate it if you were as quiet as possible as we head to my room."

Winston perked up with her admission. "I didn't know you had a kid."

"Well I don't just run around telling all my clients, Winston. Now, shhh!"

Jim awoke to find a tall, thin man in a suit standing beside his bed. A faint glow filtered in from the night-light in the hall as Jim's steady breathing turned to frantic, shallow gulps of air. *Who is this man? Why is he here? What does he want?*

"Oh, sorry. I didn't mean to wake you, little fella," the man said with an artificial tone that reminded Jim of a radio disc jockey.

"Who are you? Where's my mom?" Jim attempted to sound as calm as possible in order to keep the man from noticing that he was trembling beneath his covers.

"I'm one of your mother's friends. No need to worry – she's asleep in just the other room."

Jim was afraid to contemplate on just what exactly the term "asleep" might imply.

"I see you're into baseball," he said shooting a quick glance at Jim's glove. "You know, I also used to play baseball when I was your age. It is America's favorite pastime, after all."

"Mooooom?" Jim said barely able to raise his voice above a whisper.

"Don't worry, slugger. She's just in there," he said pointing to Jim's door and down the hallway to his mother's room.

"Mooooooooom!" Jim said raising his voice to that of a slight yell, betraying the fright he had tried to conceal.

"Aw, now don't be that way!" The man sat down on the bed next to him and placed his hand on Jim's blanket-covered leg. "I don't wanna hurt you. I just wanna be your friend."

The man's face was now only a few feet away from Jim's. He could faintly see the man's toothy grin and vaguely smell the spicy scent of his cologne.

"Winston, step away from my son right now, or I'll blow

your goddamn brains out!" Jim could just barely make out the silhouette of his mother in the doorway holding what appeared to be a small revolver.

"Ella, I was just talking with him. Right? We were just talking about baseball, weren't we?" He turned to Jim.

"Get the hell away from my son, and get the hell out of my home before I put a bullet in your head." His mother's voice was calm and steady now, but Jim recognized the fury that lay beneath.

"All right, all right," the man said as he lowered his head and slipped by her out the bedroom doorway. "You got the wrong impression, though."

She turned to Jim. "Are you all right?"

He nodded.

She followed the man through the front door with the revolver raised the entire time. The door shut behind her.

A few moments later, she came rushing back into Jim's room and sat on the bed next to him, placing the revolver on his bedside table and taking his head into her hands. She kissed his forehead and cradled him against her chest. "I'm so sorry, baby. I'm so, so sorry."

Her disheveled hair hung in strands across his face and she began to sob quietly, clinging to him. He could smell the alcohol on her breath.

"I won't let this ever happen again, sweetheart. There won't be men coming here anymore, I promise," she said as she gently rocked him back and forth in her arms.

They stayed this way for what felt like hours to Jim. Then she silently crawled beneath the covers with her dress still on and the two slept, her arm across his chest and his back pressed against her.

The next morning, Jim awoke to find his mother making breakfast, which was rare, especially when she had worked the night before. They ate together and chit-chatted about nothing, neither mentioning the events of the previous evening. She kissed him on the cheek and told him that she loved him before he went out the door to school.

Raymond met him on the stairwell as usual and they headed down to the sidewalk. A police car was parked on the street next to the housing complex, and the officer in the car stared with disapproval as they walked past.

"Ah, ol' Officer 'Harass,'" said Raymond shaking his head. "You know, I heard he once beat a man so badly he had to have his jaw wired shut."

"Well, what'd the guy do?" Jim glanced back to make sure the police car wasn't following them, but the car hadn't budged.

"Disturbed the peace."

"What's that mean?"

"My dad said that's police talk for when a black man wanders a bit too far into a white man's neighborhood." Raymond kicked a rock, imagining it to be Officer Harris's head. "It's a damn shame, if you ask me."

The two continued on towards school sharing, as well as inventing, other grotesque rumors about Officer Harris's brutality until they parted ways to their separate classrooms. For Jim, school was always a private hell; he wasn't lucky enough to share classes with Raymond, so every day he simply tried his best to go unnoticed. It rarely worked. At lunch he sat alone, and sometimes the other kids threw their Oreos at him, but he simply shrugged it off. Humiliation was better than a beating. He knew, since he'd had his share of those as well.

The long-anticipated final bell rang and Jim was free, at least for the weekend. He avoided the mob of children stampeding out the front doors by escaping through a side exit. He waited for Raymond in their usual meeting place but he never showed. After half an hour, Jim gave up and began walking home without him, assuming he must have gotten after-school detention again.

And on a Friday, too! Man, that's the worst, Jim thought.

As Jim made his way through one of the more affluent black communities of Arish, he saw a young light-skinned black man in a button-down shirt standing on the sidewalk reading a book aloud to a few people that had gathered. "And he said unto them, go ye into all the world, and preach the gospel to every creature. He that believeth and is baptized shall be saved, but he that believeth not shall be damned. And these signs shall follow …"

Jim thought this all sounded vaguely familiar; it was the type of language he'd heard in church services, though he'd only been once or twice and never really understood what was being said. The man spoke with such confidence that Jim actually stopped and listened. After a few minutes, the man closed the book and prayed. When he was done, several people gathered to thank him before dispersing. Jim tried to make a clean getaway but a hand gripped his shoulder.

"Hey young gun, I saw you walk up as I was coming to a close. You live around here?" It was the man who'd been speaking earlier.

"No. I live downtown."

"Well, I knew I hadn't seen you before. I've been visiting this area for the past week. I'm from New Life Church. You know, the one on Colonial Hill?"

Jim simply shook his head and started walking.

"Hey, no need to run off just yet. Can I ask you a quick but important question?"

Jim shrugged. "I guess so, but my mom's probably expecting me home soon."

"That's fine, I won't keep you long." He started rummaging through a messenger bag that hung around his shoulder. "Ah, here they are."

He removed two small pamphlets and looked at Jim intently, then continued, "If you were to die today, do you know where you'd go?"

"Heaven, I hope," Jim said with an uncomfortable smile.

The look on the man's face revealed that he was unamused. "Yes, but do you know for sure?"

"I don't think anyone can know that for sure."

"Oh, but you *can*, son, you can!"

Jim could hear the excitement rising in the man's voice.

"Have you accepted our Lord and Savior, Jesus Christ, into your heart? That's the only way you can know for sure."

"I've heard of him."

Jim had heard of Jesus before. Occasionally Raymond and Stevie and the other boys at the complex would get in arguments over who would win in a fight. Jesus or Superman? Or any other superhero they could come up with that day. Jim had begun to think of him as any other superhero, except for the fact that he'd never seen any comic books about him.

"Well, did you know that he loves you so much that he died so you could have everlasting life? I don't know about you, but I know none of my friends would do that much for me."

Jim simply stood in silence. This sounded like a speech the man had made many times before, but Jim was afraid to interrupt him and have to awkwardly stand there any longer than possible.

"Well, if you promise me that you'll read these, I won't keep you any longer." He extended the two pamphlets to Jim. "Can you promise me that?"

"Yeah, I guess I can do that."

The man placed them in Jim's hand and said, "If you want to know more, I'd love for you to pay us a visit at New Life Church on Sunday morning. Make sure to bring your mom, too." The man smiled and shook Jim's hand over-enthusiastically. "It was nice talking with you, young gun."

Jim cracked a half-smile and quickly turned away. He glanced at the two pamphlets as he continued down the street in the direction of his neighborhood. The first was titled "What Jesus Did for You" and the second was called "The Evil Among Us." He decided to look at them later, so he folded them up and slipped them into his front pocket.

When he made it home he noticed Stevie and the two other boys, Al and Edmund, sitting at the bottom of the stairwell talking – they sounded upset. "Hey half-breed, did you hear what happened to your buddy Raymond?" said Al as Jim approached.

"No. He didn't walk with me after school like he usually does," said Jim, ignoring their hateful looks.

"Old Officer 'Harass' arrested Raymond's dad," added Stevie.

"What for?" said Jim.

"What the hell do you think for?" said Stevie.

"My mom said it was because he was accused of robbing a white woman's house uptown," replied Edmund.

"Of course that's what they want you to think. He's gonna go to jail for it whether he's guilty or not," interjected Stevie.

"Social services came and took Raymond out of class today. I heard he's gonna go stay with an aunt in Mississippi."

Jim suddenly recalled Officer Harris's car parked outside of the housing complex that morning. Now he knew why it had been there. He felt sick to his stomach. He stepped past the boys and headed up the stairwell.

"Yeah, you better run, Oreo, before we beat the white out of you!" said Stevie followed by a bitter laugh.

Jim made his way up the stairs to his apartment, forgetting to knock before entering through the front door. His mother sat at the kitchen table smoking a cigarette and listening to a radio news report about the spread of communism in America. She blew a puff of smoke into the air and said, "How was your day, honey?"

He shook his head without speaking and headed back to his bedroom. He fell onto his bed and cried himself to sleep. Around eight o'clock, his mother brought him dinner and unsuccessfully tried to get him to talk about what was bothering him. She eventually gave up, collected his plate, and kissed him goodnight, turning out the light.

The morning sunlight streamed across Jim's face, causing him to stir awake. He felt better and for a moment wondered if the previous day had actually been nothing more than a bad dream. He stumbled to the bathroom in his underwear, then made himself a bowl of cereal in the kitchen. From the kitchen table he noticed his mother asleep on the couch with an empty bottle of cheap wine on the coffee table next to her. He hoped she hadn't been drinking because of him. He took a blanket from her bed and draped it over her, then headed back to his room.

As he lay on his bed he glimpsed the corner of one the

pamphlets the street preacher had given him sticking out of his jeans pocket. He removed both of them and looked over the one titled "What Jesus Did for You." It told the story of Jesus Christ who was born of a virgin, which, it explained in a side-note, meant he had no father but God. Through a series of illustrations with captions, it explained how he grew up among the poor and befriended the outcasts of society. Jim felt a chill run through him as he realized the parallels the story held with his own life. It went on to tell of Jesus's persecution and the sacrifice he made on the cross so all could have salvation and enter Heaven. It ended with instructions on how to perform what it called "The Sinner's Prayer."

Jim had never prayed for anything more than his own wish fulfillment, but he knew that he wanted to go to Heaven. He held the pamphlet open and mouthed the words. As he came to the "Amen" he felt a wave of relief come over him. He hoped God had been listening, since no one else was around to hear him.

He put down the pamphlet and picked up the next one entitled "The Evil Among Us." This one told of a fallen angel named Lucifer who often masquerades as an angel of light in order to deceive the followers of Christ. It said that he "influences people to become liars, thieves, murderers, and fornicators." Jim didn't know what the last word meant, but he knew it must've been pretty bad based on the ones that came before it. It went on to say that Lucifer – or the Devil, as he was often called – was the reason for all of the bad things in the world. Jim wasn't sure of this, but he did know that horrible things occurred around him every day and things only seemed to be getting worse, considering what happened to Raymond and his father the day before.

Jim's mother poked her head in the room and said,

"Would you like to go to the flea market with me today? We can get something to cheer you up." She still looked a little frazzled from her night on the couch, but her smile was genuine.

"Yeah, I'd like that," said Jim.

"All right. Well, let's get cleaned up then." She left his doorway and headed down the hall. Then he heard water running in the bathtub.

They were at the flea market by early afternoon. Jim loved looking at all the strange and interesting things people sold there. They even had an ice cream stand, so Jim and his mother ate ice cream cones as they meandered through the various stalls. Jim's favorite was a vendor that specialized in old Batman comics that he flipped through while his mother was preoccupied with the man selling puppies. She'd always wanted a dog, but she knew they didn't have the time or the money to spend on such a luxury as a pet.

By the end of the day Jim had made out like a bandit with two comics, a Davy Crockett-style coonskin hat, and a bag of plastic army men, all of which helped to significantly lift his spirits. His mother had bought a new dress and kitchen utensils. The sun dipped into the horizon, casting a pink-orange glow over everything as they left the fairgrounds where the flea market was held. *God must've heard my prayer this morning,* he thought.

"You know, you're a pretty good mom," Jim said as they ascended the steps to their apartment.

"Well, I'm glad you think so," she said, ruffling his hair a bit with her free hand.

She opened the door and Jim went back to his room with his new toys as she sat her things down on the kitchen table and started preparing dinner for the two of them. Jim set up the army men around his bed and acted out different battle scenarios for them. Soon his thoughts drifted back to Raymond and his father. What was going to happen to Raymond? Would he ever see him again? Was this the work of the Devil?

He lay on his bed contemplating what his life would be like without his best friend as he listened to his mother hum an old tune to herself in the kitchen. Why didn't God stop this from happening to Raymond, or was God even able to? Wasn't He powerful enough to do something as small as that if He was capable of sending people to Heaven or Hell? Or was this some sort of test for Jim to see if he truly believed in Him?

There was a loud crash in the kitchen as his mother screamed and a masculine voice yelled, "Police!" Then he heard a pot clang against the floor and a series of loud thuds followed by his mother crying. Jim stood up and slowly ventured out into the hallway towards the kitchen. From the doorway that connected the living room to the hallway, Jim could see Officer Harris pressing his mother against the linoleum floor with his knee grinding into her back. She was sobbing uncontrollably, and a thin stream of blood ran from her nose.

From above, Officer Harris said, "I'm arresting you for solicitation, you little whore. Now stop crying, before I give you a real reason to!"

Jim could feel a protective anger rising within him, mixing with the fear that presently kept him frozen in the doorway. His mother's desperate eyes locked on him and she screamed, "Don't watch, Jim! Go to your room! Please, don't watch, Jim!"

Without looking up at him, Officer Harris said, "Listen to your mother, boy! You don't need to see this!"

Jim's thoughts jumbled together. He imagined Raymond's father on the floor, just as his mother currently was, with Officer Harris's knee in his back. All at once he knew the helplessness that Raymond must've felt knowing that his father was going away and there was nothing anyone could do to stop it. Images of the Devil from the pamphlet ran through his mind, along with an accumulation of all the horrible things he'd seen in his short life. *There's evil among us … one who's responsible for every bad thing that's ever happened to me … he masquerades as an angel of light.*

Jim no longer had to believe in the Devil on faith, for he was there before his very eyes, brutalizing his mother. He brought nothing but pain and suffering to everyone he encountered. Jim couldn't allow it anymore. Every fiber in him screamed that this was wrong, that it had to be stopped. He knew what he had to do.

Without a word Jim turned from the doorway and passed down the hall into his mother's room as if guided by some unseen force. He opened the second dresser drawer and reached beneath her socks … .

Ella's face stung as it was pressed against the cold linoleum; the bastard had most likely broken her nose. Officer Harris dug his knee deeper into her back as he brought her wrists up and snapped the handcuffs around them. From the floor she could see that Jim had returned to the doorway, but there was something different about the way he stood. It seemed more the stance of a man and less like her little boy. His legs were spread apart, almost as if in a defensive manner, and his arms were level with his shoulders. In his hands was her revolver ….

Outside all was quiet. There was no wind to rustle the leaves, no dogs barking, only silence. Then there were three muffled pops. Then silence unabated.

PULP MYTHOLOGY

S he sat in the back booth of the diner with an unlit cigarette hanging loosely from her lips and one hand shoved in the pocket of her leather jacket, tightly gripping the snub-nosed .38 revolver as she waited for the woman to show. Her eyes gazed out the window over the wet pavement of the nearly empty parking lot. The waitress eyed her suspiciously as she made her way over.

She knew she must be quite a sight, even aside from the green hair cut into a messy mohawk that partially hung in her eyes and the studded jacket. There was now a puffy black eye and a fat lip to accompany her already attention-grabbing looks.

"Rough night?" asked the waitress as she removed the notepad and pencil from her apron.

She laughed with a lack of enthusiasm. "Yeah, you could say that."

"Now you don't have any intentions of lighting that up in here, do you honey?"

She smiled at the peculiarity of the question, withdrew the cigarette from her lips with her left hand, and placed it behind her ear. All the while never lifting a finger from the gun in her jacket pocket. "No, just knowing it's there will help calm me."

The waitress gave her a wink and a nod, "Well that's quite all right, as long as we have an understanding. Our owner's father who used to smoke two packs a day just died from lung cancer, so he doesn't allow smoking in any of his establishments anymore. Probably an overreaction that's gonna hurt business but hey, I don't make the rules, I just enforce them. So what can I get you tonight?"

"I'll start off with a coffee. Black. I'm waiting for someone."

"One black coffee coming up, sweetheart."

The waitress turned around and got the coffeemaker brewing a fresh pot. She heard the door chime as someone entered and she turned to see a tall, redheaded woman in a form-fitting, green dress with a large purse slung over her shoulder approaching her. Leaf had to admit she was more than a little impressed. The lady was a knockout; she usually didn't go for the prissy-looking bitches, but exceptions could be made now and then.

"Are you Bennie's friend? Miss Cartwright?" asked the redhead.

"That'd be me. Sit your pretty little ass in that booth and we'll have a talk," she said with a smile as she bit her lip ring in a suggestive manner.

Okay, cool it, Leaf. This woman probably intends on killing you before the night is through; she's not interested in going to bed with you.

The redhead set her purse in the booth beside her and got straight to the point. "If you know where Bennie is, tell him that if he returns our property now there will be no repercussions. If he keeps us waiting, though, he is endangering himself and everyone he cares about, including yourself, Miss Cartwright."

"'Leaf' is just fine," she said, appearing unaffected by the woman's threats. "So that's your deal, huh? Return your stuff or you're going to kill us? Not even going to butter me up a little bit? I've seen jackhammers with a more subtle touch."

"Well, Miss Cart … Leaf, if you prefer," she said with a

malicious grin. "We happen to be on a rather tight schedule, so forgive me if I don't have time for common niceties. Your friend Bennie's theft has upset many years of planning for us."

"First of all," Leaf interjected, "I don't know where Bennie is. I'm still trying to find him myself, and second, it might be helpful to know what it is he took. So, when and if I locate him, I'll know what to return to you."

The waitress set a steaming cup of coffee down in front of Leaf and then turned to the redhead. "And what can I get for you, darling?"

"Nothing. I'm fine," said the redhead coldly without making eye contact with the waitress.

"Excuse my friend's manners … Debbie, is it?" said Leaf as she glanced at the waitress's name tag. "She's had a really rough night as well. She just had her heart broken by a no-good man."

The waitress perked up. "Isn't that a damn shame?" She slapped her hands down on the table and leaned in close to the redheaded woman. "Some of these men around here just don't know how to treat a lady, do they?"

The redhead sat there quietly without responding, growing more annoyed by the second.

The waitress looked at Leaf and said, "That bastard isn't the one that gave you the shiner there, is it?"

Leaf could hardly contain her amusement. "As a matter of fact, it is."

The waitress pursed her lips angrily and began shaking her head, "I knew it, I just knew it. My friends think I'm crazy but I've always said, 'A man that'll break your heart'll just as soon as break your nose.'"

Leaf couldn't keep from snickering and the waitress eyed

her with distrust, now suspecting she was being made fun of. Leaf regained her composure and responded with complete seriousness, "Don't worry, Debbie. I knocked him flat on his ass for it. He'll think twice before putting his hand on either one of us again."

Debbie smiled. "All right, now that's what I like to hear. I—"

"On second thought, I'll have the number two with a side of eggs and some coffee," the redheaded woman blurted out in a desperate attempt to derail the conversation.

"Well, all right, darling. No need to get all excited. Coming right up." The waitress rolled her eyes at Leaf as she wrote down the order on her notepad and sauntered off to the kitchen.

The redhead shot a look at Leaf that was sharp enough to cut diamonds. "May I ask why you did that?"

Leaf shrugged and smirked. "Figured it'd piss you off. Worked, didn't it?"

"I believe you've mistaken me for someone else. I'm not the type of person you want to play games with." Her facial expression was intensely serious and something in her eyes told Leaf she truly might not want to anger this woman.

"As for your request for more information," she continued, "I'll oblige. The item your friend stole was of great historical significance. It is a mysterious, sacred relic to many people that is believed to possess god-like powers. We simply refer to it as the Artifact. It belonged to the Roman Emperor Nero until his death in 68 CE. Afterwards it disappeared for many centuries, resurfacing in the Middle Ages when it was taken into the care of the Knights Templar Order. It was then lost to history once again, though there were rumors of it being in the subterranean vaults beneath Rosslyn Chapel in Scotland for a time.

"Anyway, several years ago my associates and I learned of a potential sighting of the Artifact in Eastern Europe. So we sent a crew over to investigate and it turns out it was legitimate. Finally, it was within my grasp and it was due to arrive by cargo ship to the Lunsa Chito docks tonight. Then your friend Bennie interfered, so you can imagine why I'm so eager to have it returned." She ended with an exasperated sigh and placed both hands on the table, one on top of the other.

Leaf nodded her head, considering all that she'd been told. "Okay, okay. That all makes sense, but I do have one question though."

The redhead glared at her skeptically, sensing a smart aleck response coming. "And that would be?"

"So you're basically the bourgeois arm of the Mob that deals in black market art and collectibles? Doesn't that sorta conflict with your whole street-tough reputation?" Leaf did her best Mafioso impression, "'Yo Tony, hurry up and break his legs so we can further discuss the intricacies of Mozart's Ninth Symphony.' I mean, is it just me or is that really as lame as it sounds?"

It was obvious that the woman was unamused. The waitress stepped in. "Honey, we're all out of egg—"

"You aren't dealing with some fucking two-bit, zoot suit-wearing gangsters here!" she roared, yanking a weapon from her purse that resembled brass knuckles with metallic prongs protruding from it. There was a sudden flash of blue-green light that shot through the waitress, her smoldering body collapsed to the ground as a bevy of rapid-fire bursts of light tore throughout the diner. Leaf dropped to the floor, covering her head in her arms as fluorescent aqua beams ripped through the counter, the cash register, and unsuspecting patrons.

When the screaming ceased, Leaf heard the dwindling drone of what she hoped was a depleted power cell in the weapon. The redhead had not broken eye contact with her throughout the entire hellish ordeal. Thick smoke filled the diner and small fires had broken out all over the place.

"You've got until 6 A.M., then we start going house to house killing everyone until we find it. If you alert the authorities we will murder the entire police force of this little Podunk town of yours, then proceed unobstructed. I get the feeling that you're going to take me as a woman of my word now?" she said calmly, lowered the strange weapon as a faint trail of smoke rose from it, and casually tossed it back into her purse.

Leaf was still on the floor with her arms over her head. "Yes, I believe you."

The redhead smiled. "Good. We'll be waiting for you down at the docks. See you soon, Miss Cartwright." Then she picked up her purse, turned around, stepped over the crumpled body of the waitress, and strolled out the front doors of the diner. A large shard fell from one of the shattered pane glass doors as they swung shut behind her.

Leaf rose to her feet, dusting plaster and glass from her leather jacket. She eyed the destroyed diner around her and then removed the .38 revolver and shook her head. *Doesn't do much good if you don't actually use it, Leaf.*

She'd been completely taken off guard by the woman's looks and demeanor, which was probably exactly what she'd intended. She looked at the waitress's body, the dead customers, and the cook slumped over the kitchen counter. She could've saved them if she'd been more observant, but there was nothing that could be done now. As she made her way toward the front of the diner, the overhead sprinklers cut on.

Leaf stepped out into the humid Mississippi air, drenched as a sewer rat. Her matted green mohawk was now clumped to one side of her head. *One thing's for sure, I've got to find Bennie and I've got to find him fast.* She shook her head despondently. *How in the hell did things get like this?*

SEVERAL HOURS EARLIER

Leaf chained her bicycle to the street light in front of her apartment complex. She'd come to the conclusion that her parents were a lost cause. They'd never understand her any more than she'd understand quantum field theory or trigonometry. They felt she was completely wasting her potential working as a package handler at the Lunsa Chito Shipping Docks, but she had no aspirations of climbing the corporate ladder as they had. She loved being able to work with her hands and the coarse demeanor of the rough men she worked alongside.

Her mother and father had had big plans for her future involving socially prestigious colleges and the Young Republicans organization, but Leaf was having none of it. She wasn't dumb, but school had always bored her. So when she landed the job at the docks she emancipated herself, dropped out of high school, and moved in with a Native American hippie who called himself Nashoba.

Nashoba was the one that had given her the moniker of "Leaf." He'd said it had something to do with how green her aura was and the spirit of the nearby Leaf Creek, but she figured he'd probably had one too many puffs off his peace pipe. Nonetheless, she liked it and had her name legally changed from "Jenny" to "Leaf" a few weeks later. She'd enjoyed living with Nashoba for a time but moved out after he grew obsessed with a repressed memory of an alien abduction during his childhood.

She climbed up the stairs and latched the door behind her, still fuming from the argument with her parents. It was her birthday so she'd taken the evening off and decided against better judgment to go see them. After a surprisingly pleasant half hour of cake and small talk, they resumed their usual interrogation of her fashion, sexuality, and politics.

"Jenny, is it really necessary to have metal sticking out of your face? And why in God's name would you leave the house wearing a shirt advertising Circle Jerks on it?"

"Please tell me this whole being into girls thing is just another phase of yours."

"You better be joking about being a Communist, young lady. President Reagan and our troops are the only thing keeping those Commies from invading this country and making you give up everything you own."

She'd left without saying goodbye and rode her bike back to the apartment. *At least they had the courtesy to wait a while before they started in on me this time. That's an improvement,* she thought. She curled up on the couch with her cat, Bastet, popped a cigarette in her mouth, and was about to light it when the phone rang.

Now who the hell is calling me this late?

The telephone rang again. "All right, all right I'm coming." She put the cigarette behind her left ear and went to the phone as it rang a third time. *Maybe Mom and Dad want to apologize for the way things went earlier. Haha, now that's a good one, Leaf!*

She removed the phone from its cradle. "Hello?"

"They're coming after me. They're gonna kill me, Leaf."

The voice on the other end was low and frantic.

"What? Who—"

"It doesn't matter if I give it back. They'll kill me just to keep me from talking, I know it."

"Is that you, Bennie?"

"..."

There was several seconds of tense silence, then the line went dead.

"What was that all about?" she asked Bastet, who was staring up at her as she rubbed her side against Leaf's leg.

I'm pretty sure that was Bennie. It sure sounded like him, but I have no idea what he was talking about. She stood quietly winding the telephone cord back and forth over her fingers as she thought. *And why did he sound so scared? Bennie's a goody two-shoes. It's not like he'd be involved in a drug deal gone wrong or anything. Besides, isn't he supposed to be working tonight?*

She didn't know where the call was placed from so she decided to try his apartment. She dialed the number. It rang several times before someone picked up.

"..."

"Bennie? Is that you?"

"..."

There was no response, only more silence, but she knew someone was listening to her on the other end of the line. She hung up the phone. Something very bad was unveiling itself. All she knew was that Bennie was in trouble and he needed her help. She hoped she could make it to his place before whoever it was that picked up had left. Luckily, he didn't live far. She grabbed her baseball bat that was propped next to the door on the way out. Leaf had never used it for its intended purpose but rather as a way to scare off any door-to-door salesmen or evangelists brave enough to try her.

She skid to a stop outside of Bennie's apartment. The lights were out but she could see the dim beam of a flashlight moving around inside. She lowered her bike to the pavement and slipped the baseball bat out from underneath her studded belt. Without a sound, she ascended the steps to his third floor apartment and eased the door open. Broken glass, papers, and opened boxes of food littered the floor.

As she turned the corner to the living room she saw two men dressed in black with flashlights wearing ski masks. One had his back to her and the other was preoccupied with going through the old trunk next to Bennie's sofa. She raised the bat, preparing to bring it down on the head of the man with his back to her, and then the guy going through the trunk looked up.

"Jerry, watch out!" he screamed.

The man with his back to her turned around and slugged her hard in the eye. She fell back against the wall as he grabbed her by the shoulders attempting to restrain her. Leaf used the end of the bat as a jousting rod and rammed it into his stomach, bringing him to his knees. The guy at the trunk pulled a gun out on her. She swung the bat into his outstretched arm and there was a sickening crack as his forearm bent unnaturally and his revolver was sent flying across the room. He howled in pain, cradling his arm.

Ouch! Guess he's gonna be switching to his left hand next time he jerks off, she thought.

A fist slammed into her jaw and she stumbled backwards. Jerry was back on his feet again, ready for round two. It was time to put him down for good. She clubbed him in the left kneecap and then brought it down on his head as he slumped to the floor.

She quickly redirected her attention to his partner as he turned and ran through the open sliding glass door leading out to the balcony and dove over the railing. Leaf wondered if he recalled they were on the third floor as she heard him hit the ground below. She stepped out and peeked over the railing in time to see him hobble off into the wooded area behind Bennie's apartment complex. She returned to the living room. The man on the floor hadn't moved. She hoped she hadn't killed him since she didn't feel like having to explain herself later in court. She noticed the subtle rise and fall of his chest.

Leaf remembered his partner's revolver and gave Jerry a quick pat-down. She felt slightly guilty upon discovering he wasn't carrying. *Hey, you never know – maybe he doesn't need a weapon because he's a world-class martial artist, which would entirely justify use of a baseball bat against him.* She doubted that, though, considering his friend's bumbling response and the relative ease with which she overpowered them.

She flipped on the lights and found his partner's snub-nosed .38 lying on the opposite end of the room beneath the giant Confederate flag Bennie proudly displayed as the focal point of his living room. She smiled, considering the idiosyncrasies of her relationship with Bennie. On paper it seemed that a friendship between the two of them would never work but, fortunately, life rarely abided by compatibility checklists.

Bennie was a "good ol' boy," no doubt about it, but he

wasn't like the ignorant rednecks that had harassed Leaf throughout high school. In fact, they'd become friends after he stepped in to stop a group of teenage boys from tormenting her for being the weird kid in class. Bennie was a conservative Christian who considered himself to be part of a dying breed of Southern gentlemen. He valued the culture and traditions of the South but didn't feel the need to enforce those standards and views on others. She had to admit he could be a little stuffy and old-fashioned at times, but Leaf adored him regardless.

She picked up the revolver and opened the chamber; it was fully loaded with six rounds. She stuffed it into the right pocket of her leather jacket. Leaf was by no means an expert in firearm use, but her father was a bit of a gun enthusiast and had insisted on her accompanying him to the firing range several times in her teens. She knew how to handle a weapon, and since she didn't know exactly what to expect from these people Bennie was involved with she decided it was a good idea to keep it on her.

If Bennie had called her from his apartment then he obviously was no longer here and she didn't know where to find him. Maybe someone at the docks knew something about what was going on or where he was. She considered interrogating the unconscious man for info but she'd hit him pretty hard. She hoped she hadn't accidentally put him into a coma.

Leaf grabbed a bag of frozen peas from Bennie's freezer and held them to her face as she dialed the number to the department she and Bennie typically worked in. A woman answered. "Lunsa Chito Shipping Docks, how may I help you?"

Leaf didn't recognize the voice of the receptionist. "Is Carol off tonight? Who am I speaking to?"

"Um … this is Sharon. Carol called in sick this evening. I'm the fill-in."

The woman was lying. *They'd never be able to get a fill-in with that short of notice; the warehouse manager would've manned the phones instead.* It was clear that she'd just made up an excuse on the spot. Leaf decided against being coy and played it straight with her instead. "Let's cut the shit, what's going on? What do you guys want with Bennie?"

The woman was unprepared for Leaf's candor and it showed in her tone. "Who is this?"

"This is Bennie's friend, Leaf. He called me saying someone wanted to kill him, so I want to know why."

The woman replied with a calm, measured quality to her voice. "No one has to get hurt, we—"

"Oh, really?" Leaf interjected. "That's funny, because one of your boys just pulled a gun on me when I caught the two of them ransacking Bennie's apartment. I'd put him on and let him tell you all about it, but he doesn't seem to be in a talkative mood right now. I'm sorry, you were saying?"

The woman got to the point this time. "Your friend has something that belongs to us. Let's meet up and we can make a deal."

"All right, but I choose the place. I'm not going to walk into an ambush. You guys have already tried to kill me once tonight. Let's meet at Sal's Diner. It's on the corner of Wyatt and—"

"I know where it is," the woman said. "What time?"

"I'm heading over now so I'll be there in about ten minutes. I'll get us a booth so we can get nice and cozy," said Leaf with thinly veiled sarcasm.

"Charming," she responded dryly. "How will I know it's you?"

Leaf snickered. "I tend to get noticed pretty easily in this town. You'll know when you see me." The phone hung up abruptly on the other end. She hoped she'd made the right decision, but she needed to know what was going on if she was going to help Bennie. She took one last look at Bennie's apartment and the unconscious man on the floor, then stepped out the front door.

****

Leaf shivered as she pedaled back to her apartment on her bike. It was still humid and in the upper 80s but she was soaked from her boots to her bright, green hair. She knew she didn't have much time to find Bennie, but all she could think about was getting into some dry clothes. Police sirens and a fire engine sounded somewhere in the distance, no doubt heading for the war zone formerly known as Sal's Diner.

What kind of a weapon was that? she wondered. She'd never seen anything like it. Small and compact, yet extremely powerful. She had no idea how she and Bennie were going to make it out of this alive. They'd been in some trouble before, usually due to Leaf's temper and smart mouth, but Bennie was normally the stable, responsible one who bailed her out, whether it be from jail or an outnumbered fistfight. Now, compared to what he'd just dropped in her lap, anything she'd done seemed like childish mischief.

Always got to go for the gold no matter what you're doing, eh, Bennie-boy?

She glanced down at her wristwatch. It was almost two in

the morning; she had four hours before that redheaded psychopath started murdering everyone in town. Leaf slammed on her brakes and came to a halt in the middle of the street.

"Well, shit!"

She was only two blocks from her apartment but there was absolutely no time to spare. She needed to find Bennie immediately, wet clothes be damned. He most likely called her to meet up with him. So where would he have gone? He didn't have family nearby anymore. His parents lived several hours away in Birmingham and her parents would've freaked and called the cops if he showed up on their doorstep in the middle of the night looking for her. No, he was smart. He'd pick some place that only the two of them would think of. Some place that held some special significance for them – he was always sentimental like that.

Then it came to her. *Of course! He went to TJ's.*

TJ's was an arcade they used to hang out at for hours each day after class. Even when the place closed down after the gaming industry crash, they still found themselves using it as a place to kill time and reminisce. It was also a fun place to take the new kids late at night, filling their heads with urban legends of ghosts and child murderers. They would carefully orchestrate things to when the storyteller reached the climax of the tale the other one would jump out of the darkness and scare the bejesus out of the kid. Leaf smiled just thinking about it. She spun her bike around and rode down the hill toward the abandoned strip mall.

The mall looked worse since the last time she'd seen it. The broken windows were now boarded up and a good portion of the building was covered in graffiti. As she got closer, she saw the storefront curb was littered with cigarette butts and broken beer bottles. Obviously, it was a hangout place for the high schoolers nowadays as well. She went one-by-one checking each of the boards until she found the one she was looking for.

Yep, he's been here all right.

The large piece of plywood hung loosely by a single nail at its top-center so it still appeared to cover the window, but it was able to swing freely to the left or right, allowing access to the inside of the arcade. It was a trick that Bennie had come up with to conceal their presence from the casual passersby or nightly patrol car. She picked up her bike and lifted it through the window frame, holding the plywood clear with her back. She leaned her bike against the inside wall and turned around to see Bennie standing there with his arms out.

"Happy birthday! … " he exclaimed, embracing her. As he drew back from her, his tone was glummer. "… It's the end of the world."

Bennie was wearing a sleeveless Lynyrd Skynyrd shirt and an Ole Miss Rebels cap that he was rarely seen without. He hadn't attended the college but felt that supporting the football team was a point of local pride. They walked into the light of a lantern he'd set up in one of the game rooms in the back and he got a good look at her black eye and fat lip. "Good god, what happened to your face?"

She laughed and said, "Thanks, Bennie. It's nice to see you, too!"

Bennie wasn't amused. "I'm serious, Leaf. Who did that to you?"

She shrugged. "Just some assholes I found turning your apartment inside out. Believe me, they look worse than I do. One of them's going to have to permanently alter his golf swing and the other one … will hopefully be waking up soon."

He lowered his head. "I'm sorry, Leaf. You went there looking for me after I called you, didn't you? I didn't want you to get hurt. I just didn't know where to turn and I was scared. I still am, I'm holding it together a little better than I was a few hours ago, but we're in way over our heads here."

She stared back at him, knowing full well the danger they were in. "You don't have to tell me that, Bennie. I just watched one of them murder an entire diner full of people about an hour ago, simply to demonstrate how serious she was about finding that Artifact or whatever it is that you took from them."

Bennie's face went pale. "I … I never wanted anyone to get hurt, but I knew they had to be stopped. I should've known they would do something like this when they got desperate. They'll kill anyone and everyone to get back the Artifact."

"Bennie, they're going to kill a lot more people if you don't give them what they want. You need to start telling me what's going on, who these people are, and what you stole from them. You're the most law-abiding, honest person I know. How in the hell did you get mixed up in all of this?"

A long-held sigh escaped his lips as he began. "A few weeks ago I was pulling my usual all-nighter at the docks. You were off that night, for some reason or another."

"Was that the night I went to the Black Flag show?" Leaf asked, removing the cigarette from behind her left ear. She discovered it was still soaked from the diner's fire sprinklers when it fell apart in her hand as she was preparing to light it.

"Yeah, I think so. Anyways, this black BMW pulls up and this redheaded woman and two guys that looked like wannabe CIA agents step out. Mike was on that night, and they start telling him about how they have a very important shipment arriving in a few weeks. We assume they're from the museum that placed the shipment order and their IDs checked out and everything. Mike thinks they're a bit uptight, but other than that it's no big deal. He takes their number and tells the lady he'll let her know the night it arrives … "

Leaf checked her pockets and removed the half-empty pack of Camels she had. She opened it to see they were waterlogged as well. "Goddamnit! All I want is one cigarette – is that so much to ask?"

Bennie stared at her, startled by the sudden outburst.

She dropped the pack of cigarettes on the ground and looked up at him. "Sorry. Please continue."

He shook his head in a mock judgmental manner she'd seen many times. "So while the redhead is gabbing away to Mike, I overhear the two guys by the car who are unaware I'm standing behind the shipping container they parked next to and they're saying some of the weirdest crap I've ever heard. 'Our Lord Nero this, Our Lord Nero that, something, something ancient Artifact, and the heralding of a new era.' You know, some scary Book of Revelations, end-of-the-world type stuff.

"By this point I'm beginning to think these guys sound a lot more like one of those crazy satanic cults you hear about on the news than some harmless museum curators. When they leave, I try to get Mike to tell me about them but he writes it off and says they're just some snooty history buffs worried about a supposedly priceless something or other, but I ain't buying it. So when my shift ends I head to the library and ask for any books about Nero and cults, but don't find much connecting the two.

"After a couple of hours I'm about to give up and leave when this librarian walks up to me and says she has a book I might be interested in, but it's old and hard to find so it can't be checked out from the library. I can look at it and make some photocopies if I want, though. So I wait in this study room and she brings this massive, leather-bound book to me that was written in the 1800s by some Englishman, Sir Thomas Hixton. It's called *Mysteries of the Ancients* and it's a reference book about all these religious cults throughout history. So I look up Nero, and this is what I find."

He held out several pages of photocopies from the book. Leaf took them with a confused look on her face. "Why are you giving these to me?"

"Why do you think? Because I want you to read them."

She sighed dramatically. "We don't have time for this, Bennie. Just tell me what it says."

"You won't believe me unless you read it for yourself."

She shook her head. "I love you, but sometimes you annoy the crap out of me."

He smiled back at her. "Feeling's likewise, babe."

Leaf read the text aloud as Bennie stood by.

"'The Roman emperor Nero was the first great persecutor of the Christians. After the Great Fire of Rome in 64 A.D., he accused them of arson and used it as an excuse to label them enemies of the state, executing them on a widespread scale. Many Christians and Roman citizens believed Nero had actually orchestrated the fire himself so that he could rebuild Rome in his own image. During the reconstruction, Nero erected great bronze statues of himself and constructed his *Domus Aurea*, or Golden House, where Roman aristocracy had lived on Palatine Hill.

"'Meanwhile, the Christian scapegoats were torn apart by wild dogs, fed to lions in gladiator matches, and tied to stakes covered in tar to be used as human torches. Nero's excessive cruelty caused sympathy among Roman citizens for the fringe religious group, though the Emperor's family did not fare much better than his enemies. He poisoned his stepbrother, had his mother stabbed to death, beheaded his first wife, and beat his pregnant second wife to death in an argument.'"

Leaf glanced up at Bennie. "Okay, I get it. Nero was an asshole."

Bennie looked back at her impatiently. "Keep reading."

"Ugggghhhh! 'The Roman Senate soon turned against their emperor and there was a plot to assassinate him. Nero got wind of it and had all the conspirators killed without trials. Then unexpectedly, at the age of thirty, Nero committed suicide by falling on his own sword. The remainder of the Roman Senate placed him under *Damnatio Memoriae*, attempting to erase him from the annals of history. His name was removed from monuments and sculptures were reworked to represent beloved historical figures. Though, in the end, their efforts were unsuccessful and his name lives on in infamy.

"'After Nero's death, some Jewish circles believed he would one day return and resume his role as tyrant and adversary of the followers of Christ. The Book of Revelations seems to cryptically reference Nero when it prophesizes that one known as the Beast, or Antichrist, will recover from a mortal wound, such as the one Nero inflicted upon himself when he fell onto his sword taking his own life. Revelations also reveals that the number of the Beast is the number of a man, which is 666, and the numerical word value of *Caesar Nero* in Hebrew is 666, another apparent reference to Nero. A third reference is made when the book says the seven heads of the Beast represent the seven hills and the capital of Nero's empire was Rome, also known as the City of Seven Hills.

"'The Roman Senate prevented Nero from being deified after his death and the remainder of his imperial cult was ostracized and driven into hiding, yet many are unaware that they have continued to this very day. Through the millennia the Cult of Nero – or Resurrection Cult, as they have come to be known – have collected personal items of the Emperor for use in secretive rituals believing that they hold great power. Similar to many Christians, the Resurrection Cult awaits Nero's return, although they are eagerly anticipating the day expecting to be rewarded with positions of power as his loyal servants. There is one item of particular importance to the cult, known as the Artifact, rumored to open the gates of Hell heralding Nero's triumphant return as a malevolent god-king.'"

Leaf stopped and said, "Okay, I read it but I still don't believe that crap. It's just a bunch of pseudo-religious nonsense by a group of homicidal whack jobs. Please tell me you didn't fall for that stuff, Bennie."

Bennie hung his head and sighed in dismay. "You're always so skeptical, Leaf. Even when the evidence is right in front of you, you refuse to think outside of the box you put yourself in."

Leaf looked at him, her blood pressure rising. "Don't you dare, Bennie. Don't make this into another one of your religious arguments. We don't have time for it. Now I have no doubt that this Resurrection Cult, or whatever they call themselves, believes they're doing the Devil's bidding, and you can believe it too if you want, but it really doesn't matter right now. All that matters is that we stop them before more people get killed."

"Maybe you'll change your mind once you've seen it." He turned around and picked up the lantern. "Come on."

Leaf followed him further into the darkness of the abandoned arcade until they reached a large room in the back with a small closet located along the rear wall. He sat the lantern on the floor and opened up the closet door. There was a familiar faint blue-green light emanating from within as he lifted the object up to his chest. It had a somewhat conical shape with a wide base, reminding her of a metallic flower bud. It stood three feet tall with small clear panels on each side covered in a type of transparent plastic or glass. A small, aqua-colored orb of light levitated at its core.

"This is the Artifact, the object they're so desperate to get their hands on. It didn't start glowing like that until a few hours ago. I think it's actually gotten a little bit brighter since the last time I looked at it. So 'Ms. Everything Has a Rational Explanation,' how do you explain that?"

"Hey, I didn't say I could explain what's going on," said Leaf, "but that doesn't mean I believe this thing's going to open the portal to Hell. I don't know what that weapon she used at the diner was either, but the two are obviously somehow connected."

Bennie frowned. "About that. I've been trying to figure out why she didn't kill you when she found out you didn't have the Artifact or know where it was, because it's risky to leave you alive with everything you know about them now."

She shrugged. "Unless she figured there was nothing I could really do to stop them."

"Or if they thought you'd eventually lead them to me and the Artifact … which you just did."

Leaf's eyes widened in fear. "No, that's impossible. No one followed me. I would've seen them."

"I wouldn't underestimate them. I'm going to check out the parking lot just to be sure," he said turning toward the front of the building, the Artifact still in his hands.

A voice rose from the darkness as a figure emerged in the low light. "Let me save you the time."

It was the redheaded woman from the diner, only now she was wearing a large metallic headdress decorated with many jagged edges and ornate serpentine creatures. She also wore an intricately designed armored breastplate fitting her like a corset as it flowed into a dress made of long, thin interwoven blades. Her eyes were covered in dark eyeshadow with the hyperrealistic image of a black star with massive, arcing solar flares painted on her forehead.

Soon others stepped out into the light, forming a semi-circle around Bennie and Leaf as they were forced against the back wall of the arcade. The other members of the Resurrection Cult wore sleeveless black cassocks with the image of the same star inlaid in white across their chests. Each carried a large pointed staff with a small glass sphere beneath its tip. The cult was predominately male, and Leaf noticed one of them limping with his right arm in a sling.

The redheaded woman looked to Leaf, revealing that malicious grin once more. "Thank you for leading us back to the Artifact, Leaf. We couldn't have done it without you."

Leaf stood silently, she couldn't believe she'd been manipulated so easily. In retrospect, their plan was painfully obvious.

The redhead turned to Bennie. "Now, if you'd be kind enough to hand the Artifact over to us before any more blood has to be shed."

Bennie held it close to his chest. "You know I'm not going to do that."

"Then *she* is going to pay the price for your defiance," she said lifting a familiar weapon in Leaf's direction.

Leaf stared back at the same chrome, multi-pointed weapon she'd seen used to murder an entire diner full of people earlier that morning. She knew there was no surviving this.

"Why her? Why don't you just shoot me and take it?" said Bennie studying her movements.

"I won't risk damaging the Artifact. Not after I've come this far."

"Then you'll just kill us both after I give it to you," said Bennie.

The sphere at the end of each cult member's staff began to faintly glow the same color as the Artifact.

The woman's voice was slightly frantic now. "That's not true. The two of you are completely insignificant in the grand scheme of things. You'd be free to go live what's left of your pointless little lives. I don't care."

"There's still something you're not telling us," said Bennie.

"TIME'S UP!" the woman screamed.

Leaf pulled the trigger of the .38 and a bullet ripped through her jacket pocket, striking the redhead in the chest. Leaf squeezed the trigger several more times. The woman fell backwards, sending a fluorescent blast into the ceiling as her weapon discharged. The spheres on each cult member's staff grew blindingly bright as they formed into an interconnected beam of light that shot forth into the Artifact in

Bennie's hands. Leaf averted her eyes as a bolt of lightning filled the room. Then everything went dark.

Leaf's eyes slowly readjusted to the dim light of the lantern. She heard heavy breathing that seemed to come from everywhere at once. The cult members had laid their staffs down and were now bowing on their hands and knees chanting, "Lord Nero has come! Praise Lord Nero!" Bennie stood before them with both of his arms outstretched, basking in their adulation. The Artifact was now at his feet as Leaf's gaze rose to Bennie's eyes, but there were only two cold, empty pools of black staring back at her.

A deafening, demonic voice that was not his own rose from Bennie's mouth. "*Nero*? I am not Nero. Nero was a spoiled mama's boy when I found him. He was merely the Vessel I chose."

Leaf tried to process what was going on and who or what had taken over her best friend, but things were happening so fast. "All right, so if you're not Nero then I guess you're supposed to be the Devil?"

The thing that was now Bennie looked at her and laughed. "The Devil? You silly, superstitious humans come up with so many interesting explanations for things beyond your level of comprehension. I am Zaltrathinius, Conqueror of the Cosmos. I have sent psychic transmitters all across the universe subjugating the lesser star systems and their species. Entire civilizations have fallen under my sway without me ever having to step a foot on their planet. No bloody invasions or costly wars – one of my transmitters simply connects with a Vessel and the battle is already won. Each world has its own religions, but my cult spans across galaxies. I am the one true God that unites them all."

Leaf put her thumb and index finger to her chin. "Wow,

Mr. Xanax, that all sounds *super* impressive. I mean, I've always wondered why Nero was one of the biggest assholes in history and now I know it's because it was actually you. I've gotta be honest, though, I've never really been that into the idea of pretentious aliens or space gods telling me how to live my life. So I'm going to have to decline the tempting offer of being one of your groveling subjects for the rest of eternity."

Zaltrathinius was unamused. "I do not respond well to being mocked by contemptuous women. You are familiar with the fates of Nero's mother and both of his wives, aren't you?"

"Why yes I am," she said, carefully concealing the revolver behind her back since she'd already blown apart the right pocket of her jacket. "I'm also aware that you already tried to conquer this planet once and you failed. Nero's dead and the Roman Empire collapsed. Now for some reason you think you're gonna have better luck two thousand years later?"

Zaltrathinius contorted Bennie's face into an unnaturally wide smile, revealing gnarled jagged teeth sprouting from his gums. Then he held out his left hand as Leaf watched his fingers form into long needle-like points. "In the time I've spent waiting for the transmitter to recharge I've made a few upgrades. Now I can manipulate the shape and structure of your primitive primate bodies. I know a couple thousand Earth years must seem like an eternity to humans, with your pathetically short life cycles, but to me it was as fleeting as a breath in the wind. Don't be misled by humanity's delusions of self-importance; in this universe, your species is truly insignificant."

Leaf watched as Bennie's limbs lengthened and his torso elongated as he grew to an unnatural height. When the transformation was complete, he was utterly unrecognizable.

There was only a twelve-foot-tall nightmarish creature in ill-fitting clothes towering over her. His facial features had been stretched back as if his face was made of rubber, his nose and hair were nonexistent, and his ears were pointed like that of a bat. The pale face studied her with a pleased expression. "Now I will do you a favor and end your suffering. Really, you should thank me for relieving you of the existential anxiety of continuing such a meaningless life."

Leaf stepped back a few feet and eyed the Artifact on the ground behind him. Her finger rested on the trigger of the revolver as she prepared to use it once again. Something stirred off to her right. She saw the redheaded woman rising to her feet. *Damn, just when I thought I was finally through with her.*

The redhead stepped in front of the creature and said, "Let me dispose of her, my Lord." She turned angrily to Leaf. "I was supposed to be the Vessel. I spent my entire life preparing for His return. Now you and your friend have ruined everything." A small stream of blood trickled out from a bullet hole in the woman's armored breastplate. At least one of her shots had made it through, but only enough to slow the woman down.

I'll have to make sure the next round really counts, she thought. She prepared to take aim when long jagged fingers burst through the redhead's chest and she was lifted high into the air. Zaltrathinius spread his fingers apart, tearing the woman in half and showering Leaf in a thick, red mist.

Leaf fell onto her back screaming, "Holy shit!"

Zaltrathinius simply smiled. "She said her life no longer served a purpose and I agreed. Plus, I want the pleasure of destroying you myself."

The massive creature lumbered forward, reaching for her

with its gore-stained fingers. She knew there was only one possibility left to stop this thing. Zaltrathinius stood above her, pinning her against the floor with his foot atop her chest. Leaf wriggled her arm out from beneath her back and held up the revolver.

"You really think that gun will stop me?" he cackled.

She eyed the back wall where the remaining cult members had huddled together in fear after seeing their resurrected god viciously tear apart the cult leader. Ironically, there seemed to be a lack of faith in their cause now that their goal was finally realized. Leaf saw the faint glow of the Artifact at their feet. She pulled the trigger. The first round was a bit off, hitting the wall to the left of the Artifact, but the second struck home. The aqua light within flickered and a sound like the crackling of electrical current filled the arcade.

Zaltrathinius stumbled backwards, crashing into an inner wall before falling to the floor. He struggled to control his limbs and get upright as if his own body was now unfamiliar. The creature spoke, no longer in the voice of Zaltrathinius but as Bennie once again. "What has he done to me, Leaf?" The creature's face was in anguish and she noticed its eyes were no longer black but those of her best friend.

Leaf got on her feet and ran to him. A bloodied claw reached for her as she approached. "Whoa, watch it, Bennie! Those things are deadly."

He began to sob. "I'm sorry. He's made me into such a freak."

She got down and cradled his head, trying to ignore the hideous face and focus solely on the friendly, familiar eyes she'd known for so many years. "It's okay, Bennie. We'll find some way to reverse it. Maybe if we destroy that thing," she said, pointing to the Artifact.

"It can't be destroyed, Leaf. You just temporarily disrupted the connection. He's still in here with me. I can feel him trying to regain control. We can read each other's thoughts, and he's pure evil. Don't tell me the Devil doesn't exist, because he's inside of me right now."

"He's an alien, Bennie, not some supernatural deity. Alien technology is causing all of this."

"No! Can't you see? It doesn't matter the means Satan employs, that's all superficial. He wants to do the Devil's bidding and bring about the end of this world. This is the Apocalypse as foretold in Revelations."

"If that's true, then where's God? Isn't he supposed to come riding in on a white horse and save us?"

Bennie shook his head. "He acts through us Leaf, just like this Devil. The early Christians were right; Nero was the Antichrist. He was going to use the Emperor of the Roman Empire to bring about the Apocalypse but his Vessel, the real Nero, found a way to stop him. The Christians knew he would return one day and now he's fulfilled that prophecy. I can stop him though, just as Nero did before."

"How, Bennie?"

He looked over to the mangled pieces of the redheaded woman's body. "The weapon she had. Bring it to me."

Leaf cradled him, carefully propping his head against the wall, and ran to find it. The weapon was still in the dead woman's hand. Leaf pried her cold fingers free from it and brought it to Bennie. "What are you going to do?"

"Hurry, Leaf! I can feel him starting to take control again."

Leaf placed the weapon in the strange grotesque hand that had once belonged to Bennie as she saw his eyes go black.

The creature started laughing as it pointed the weapon at her. The demonic voice of Zaltrathinius had returned. "As your friend said, we know each other's thoughts, and I must say I'm impressed that the Christ cult still persists. I was sure that I'd stamped them out after the Great Fire of Rome. I used their flaming carcasses as the light for my garden parties."

Leaf pulled the revolver's trigger, but there was only the sound of the hammer falling as the empty cylinders rotated around. She let the gun slip from her hand and fall to the floor.

Zaltrathinius looked at her, somewhat disappointed. "Well, I guess this is it for you. It was a valiant effort but it always ends the same for those that oppose me. Any last words?"

Leaf thought for a second then nodded her head. "Yeah … you suck."

Zaltrathinius grinned as Leaf closed her eyes and waited for the blast that would end her. Several tense seconds passed but it never came. When she reopened her eyes she saw that Zaltrathinius had turned the weapon toward himself. Then she heard Bennie's voice again.

"Nero was the first to figure it out. Zaltrathinius is nearly unstoppable, but he relies on the Vessel's will to live, which is the most basic instinct of every living creature, unless the Vessel stops resisting him and chooses to take its own life. Once the connection is severed, the Artifact will need another two thousand years to recharge before it has the power to form a link with a new Vessel.

"At first I couldn't understand why God allowed this to happen to me but now I get it. He knew I would have the courage to do what others couldn't. That's why I became the

Vessel instead of the cult leader. It was all part of God's plan. This isn't the end, Leaf. Not for you, not yet."

Leaf fell to her knees. "No Bennie, don't do this. There's gotta be another way. I already disrupted the connection once; you wouldn't be able to talk to me if I hadn't. Maybe I can stop it altogether if I try again."

He shook his head. "No, this is the only way, Leaf. I can't explain how I know it, but I do. I'm sorry."

The creature began to shake and shudder as the voice of Zaltrathinius returned. "If you do this, I'll come for her descendants and I will be relentless. I will make them suffer and that will be my number one priority above anything else."

Bennie's voice broke through again. "Leaf, you'll prepare them. The story of the Artifact will be passed down as a family heirloom. They'll be waiting and ready for his return. Promise me that you'll do it, Leaf!"

Her mind was spinning from an overload of information, discussion of the fate of her hypothetical descendants, having to witness the split personalities of this creature at war with itself, and the impending death of her best friend.

Bennie's voice cut through her mental haze. "Promise me, Leaf!"

She finally broke down as tears began to stream down her face, "Okay, okay, Bennie! I promise!"

She heard Zaltrathinius scream in anguish, then Bennie's voice whispered, "I love you, Leaf. I always have."

A blast of fluorescent light filled the room once more and Zaltrathinius's body went slack. There was a massive burning hole in the drywall where his head had been. Leaf crawled over to Bennie's deformed body and collapsed onto his chest. She didn't know how much time had passed when she'd stopped crying and lifted her head to see the cult around her. They stood solemnly with their heads bowed. She could feel the rage rising like a tidal wave inside of her. She yanked the alien weapon from Bennie's clawed hand and pointed it at them.

"Your god has abandoned you, your cult leader is dead, and my best friend is dead. I really should roast you bastards with this thing after all that you've done. It's what you deserve, but I've seen enough death tonight. Leave this city and don't ever come back. If you do, I'll be waiting for you – and I won't be so forgiving next time."

The cult members looked around at each other and realized they had no choice but to comply. She waved her hand to the front entrance. "That way so I can see you." One of them stopped and turned to the Artifact. "Don't even think about it. I'm keeping the Artifact, your staffs, and this gun or whatever it is. Now get the hell out."

Leaf watched as they exited through the door they had pried apart earlier to enter the arcade. When they were gone, she looked around trying to determine what to do next. She picked up the staffs and carried them over to her bike, and then she did the same with the Artifact. She knew it would be difficult attempting to carry these while riding her bike back home, but she figured she could manage it. She stuffed the strange weapon into the left pocket of her jacket and returned to the room in the back of the arcade.

Blood and carnage surrounded her as she looked upon the scattered remains of the redhead and Bennie's misshapen corpse. *My poor, sweet Bennie.* It felt wrong to leave him like this. He was a kind-hearted, beautiful person, but when people saw this abomination it would be remembered more than the person he truly was. No, she couldn't bear that. She would have to destroy the body so it would never be connected to him.

He deserved to at least keep his dignity if it was the last thing she could ever give to him. *Hell, I'll just burn down this whole rickety arcade. Seems fitting; this place meant more to him than it ever did to anyone else. TJ's will be your funeral pyre, Bennie.* Leaf smiled weakly as tears reformed in her eyes. *Yeah, he'd like that.*

She pulled plywood from the windows and boards from the doors and piled them onto his body. When she felt there was enough to get a fire going, she reached into her jeans and removed her Zippo. She flicked it until there was a steady flame and set one of the pieces of plywood ablaze. Leaf watched it burn for a good ten minutes until she was confident it wouldn't sputter out.

I wish I could have an ounce of the faith that you had, Bennie-boy. Who knows? Maybe you're right about the whole God and Heaven thing, and you're looking down at me smiling and shaking your head right now. I would've never believed in an ancient-mind-controlling-alien-space-conqueror if I hadn't seen it for myself, so what do I know?

In the corner of her eye, something caught her attention. It was Bennie's Ole Miss hat. She picked it up off the floor and pushed her green bangs out of her eyes as she placed the hat on top of her head. She gathered up the staffs and the Artifact and carefully balanced them across her lap as she got onto her bicycle. She turned and took one last look at the fire that was steadily consuming the inside of TJ's.

Goodbye, Bennie.

Then she pedaled her bike out the front door of the arcade and into the warm rays of the morning sun.

On the way home, she was struck with the most intense craving for a cigarette she'd ever had, so she stopped at Lunsa Chito's oldest corner store as it was opening for the day.

She quietly stood at the front counter as the elderly clerk approached. "Christ, what happened to your—"

"I know, I look like paved-over shit," she interrupted. "Can I please just get a pack of Camel Straights?"

The clerk looked at her with an apologetic face and said, "Our supply truck is running late this week, so we're actually all out right now."

Leaf stared back at him in disbelief. "You have *got* to be kidding me …"

MIDNIGHT

Another evening
Midnight crept into our bed
Now it sleeps beneath our sheets
Cold, dark feet against my legs
Oh, how I wish you'd told me
But all was left unsaid

I try to breathe or speak
But it weighs down,
Perched upon my chest
Once this place was sacred
Now black fingers weave
Their curses in my head

I want to shake you
Wake us both
Finally end this dread
But when you turn to face me
I see its eyes staring
From deep inside your head

SIREN

Gareth was deciding what to do on his day off. He'd slept until eleven simply because he could. His wife, Heather, had left for work around seven-thirty so he had the place to himself. He made a late breakfast and gazed through the kitchen window.

He saw their neighbor, Celeste, hunched over on her front porch swing with her head in her hands. Her jet-black hair hung in strands over her knees. Gareth had seen her several times, usually as she was coming home from work. He'd always waved, though he rarely received a response. Celeste and her boyfriend Damien were the youngest couple on the street, most likely in their mid-twenties from what he could tell. The majority of the residents assumed they were riff-raff, due to their black clothing and tattoo-covered skin, but Gareth wasn't one to judge.

In fact, he found Celeste's dark demeanor somewhat alluring, though he'd never admit it. He'd never had the courage to stand out or go against the grain, even though he secretly admired those that did. As a child he had always done what he was told, and growing up he never attempted to rock the boat or draw undue attention, but inside he imagined a different, more assertive version of himself. As an adult, he had taken a safe job in the most reliable career path he could find: market research analysis. Even his wife had not really involved any risk on his part; she'd been a family friend that his parents had set him up with.

Heather was an attentive spouse and a genuinely caring person. She was also a bronze-skinned beauty with blond hair, making her most guys' idea of a "perfect ten," or at least that's what his friends told him. She was the path of least resistance and when his parents suggested he propose, he honestly couldn't think of a reason not to. Life with her was by no means bad, it was just a little vanilla and their sex life reflected that as well. He sometimes wondered if Heather even knew there were positions other than missionary, but it felt selfish to complain. Most people would kill to have a life or partner like his so he felt he should be grateful for what he had.

His daydreaming was interrupted by the smell of burning eggs. He quickly pulled the skillet off the stove and stirred the eggs, hoping to save what he could. He scraped the unusable bits into the sink and ran the water to rinse it out. He returned to the window and saw Celeste's icy-blue eyes staring straight back at him. He was so startled he dropped the entire skillet in the sink. When he looked up again, he saw Celeste's back as she entered her house.

God, I'm such a child. I really hope she didn't see me jump.

A few moments later Damien threw open the front door to his and Celeste's home. He appeared to be quite angry and Gareth was able to lip-read a few colorful obscenities escaping his mouth as he yanked open the door of their beat-up Camaro. The car plowed over Gareth's mailbox as he peeled out of the driveway, and then with another screech of tires Damien was gone.

Son of a bitch didn't even slow down, thought Gareth. *Oh, well, it's not like I don't know where to find him when the time comes to pay for it.*

Gareth had already finished eating breakfast when he heard a knock at the front door. Through the peephole was the distorted image of a darkly dressed figure standing on his front porch. As the figure lifted its head, he was able to make out Celeste's features.

For some reason he hesitated opening the door. They'd never actually spoken face-to-face and he was a little frightened to let her into his life. He wasn't sure how he knew but a voice inside him said, *the moment you open this door your life is going to change.* He couldn't just leave her standing on the porch, though; she knew he was there. After all, they'd made eye contact through the window earlier.

He breathed in deeply and swung the door open wide.

Celeste spoke first. "Hi, I'm really sorry about your mailbox. Damien's got a bit of a temper."

Gareth gave her a sympathetic smile and said, "I can see that. He doesn't really seem like the type that needs to be behind the wheel when he's angry … sorry, that's probably none of my business."

"No need to apologize. You're completely right – he's a reckless idiot who just destroyed your mailbox. You have every right to say that."

Her porcelain-white features and the large expressive eyes that seemed to peer deep inside of him transfixed Gareth. He suddenly felt the overwhelming need to help her. "Are you all right? Is there anything I can do?"

She stood motionless without saying anything for several seconds and Gareth began to regret asking, thinking maybe he had crossed a line. Celeste's eyes welled with tears and her lip lightly trembled.

She held her hand over her face, looking somewhat embarrassed. "I'm sorry, he can be such an uncaring asshole sometimes. It's just nice to have someone ask me how I am for once and care about my feelings. I know I'm pathetic; I should probably just go."

She turned around, about to head for her house when Gareth reached out and put his hand on her shoulder. "No it's all right. You don't have to go. If you want I can make some coffee and we'll talk about it."

With her back to him, she slowly turned her head to the left and glanced at his hand resting on her shoulder. She spun around and faced him. "Do you really mean it?"

"Of course." He held the door with one hand and motioned her inside.

As she crossed through the doorway in front of him, he let his eyes wander over her curvy body. She wore a black flannel shirt over a tank top with a menacing band logo and skin-tight black leggings tucked into loosely tied combat boots. It was an outfit his wife wouldn't be caught dead in, and maybe that was part of its allure. He suddenly felt a twinge of guilt at the thought.

He got a pot of coffee going as Celeste watched from the couch in the living room. He leaned against the kitchen counter as he waited for the coffee to finish brewing and asked Celeste what had happened.

"Damien says that I nag him too much, but he seriously spends all of his money on pot and video games. It's like I'm raising a moody teenager sometimes. He was short on his side of the rent again. So I confronted him about it and suggested that maybe he should stop wasting his money on frivolous things and try being responsible for once. He just lost it and started yelling at me. I went outside to calm down and when I came back in he just stormed off like a child, as you saw."

Gareth shook his head and cracked a smile. "Well damn, I think Heather and I are too bored with each other to even fight anymore. Sometimes I've thought about starting an argument with her just for a little excitement."

Celeste laughed. "Be careful what you wish for. Damien and I have enough drama to go around."

The coffee had finished draining so Gareth removed the pot and poured two cups for them. "I like mine black. How do you take yours?"

"Let's just say I like my sugar with coffee and cream," she said.

He nodded his head. "Point taken."

He handed Celeste her coffee and sat down on the love-seat next to the couch.

Celeste sipped her coffee and sighed. "So … I have an embarrassing confession to make."

Gareth perked up. "Really? What's that?"

She grinned girlishly and looked up at the ceiling. "I used to rush home from work just so I could catch you doing yard work with your shirt off in the afternoons."

His face turned slightly red as he sat his cup on the coffee table. "You've got to be kidding me."

"Nope. You usually start around three-thirty and if I was lucky, your shirt came off by four."

"Well, it's good to know those mornings at the gym paid off for something." He said with a laugh. He hesitated for a moment. "Since we're being honest, I suppose I should tell you that I've found you intriguing since the first day you moved in."

"Intriguing? I'm not quite sure how to take that. Sounds kinda like how you might describe a science project or something."

He threw up his hands. "All right, all right. I'll admit I find you attractive. You just seem so different from me or anyone that I know."

She placed her coffee on the table and uncrossed her legs.

Her flannel shirt slid down, exposing one of her pale shoulders. "I don't know that we're really all that different. I'm just not as afraid to get what I want."

"Oh, really? And what is it that you want?"

She paused for a moment and stared back at him with a deadpan look on her face. Then she removed the flannel shirt, followed by her tank top and bra. She appeared to move weightlessly through the air as she eased up from the couch and stood before him in an extremely seductive manner. Her breasts were full and supple, topped with the most exquisite pink nipples he'd ever seen. He felt himself growing aroused as she leaned over, intentionally letting her breasts brush against his face, and straddled him.

Her leggings were so thin that he could feel the warmth of her thighs through his basketball shorts as she steadily moved back and forth against his rapidly hardening member. He exhaled, thinking to himself that he could still put an end to this if he just pushed her off of him … but he knew that he wouldn't. With that, he felt the last bit of his resolve crumble.

He placed one hand on the small of her back and the other on her hip and pressed her more firmly against him. They both breathed heavily as they moved in time with one another. He grabbed the back of her head, his fingers full of her hair, and kissed her passionately. He felt her hands lift up his shirt and he yanked it off entirely, eager to feel their bare chests pressed together. Shivers crawled up his spine the moment her warm skin touched his; he felt the slight perspiration between her breasts causing them to cling together. He arched his head, his lips gasping against her neck, and glimpsed the massive tattooed wings upon her back that appeared to ripple with life as she swayed to and fro.

With her knees bent toward him he was able to reach forward and slide off her combat boots. Then his hands made their way up the backs of her thighs and squeezed her firm buttocks as she grasped his shoulders and grinded against his abs. Through the leggings he could feel a damp warmth between her legs.

He whispered into her ear, "I need to be inside of you."

She stood up and grasped the top of his shorts, pulling them down around his ankles and then off into the floor. She wrapped her hand around his now throbbing erection and gently stroked it from the head to the base.

He whimpered, "Please don't tease me any longer."

A devilish grin spread across her face as she bent down and stripped off her leggings. He licked his lips as he watched her climb back on top of him, grasp him firmly, and slide him into her warmth. He bit his lower lip and held her hips as she rode him slowly, eventually building up to a rapid pace. In the throes of ecstasy his hands ran up her back and he swore he felt the smooth texture of feathers …

He laid his head between her breasts as she reclined against the armrest. He watched her chest slowly rise and fall with her breathing and thought of the ebb and flow of ocean tides. She gently ran her hands through his hair and began to softly hum a tune. He was enchanted by its melody and as he drifted off to sleep he knew there was no way back to his old life. He was now a ship crashing onto the rocks of a forbidden shore.

EVEN MORE SYMPATHY
FOR THE DEVIL

Lucifer and I sat and talked about
the ways of this world
He took a sip from his flask
And said, "I always got a bad rap for
wanting to go my own way
All I ever wanted was to
maybe start a band or something"

I replied, "That's what you get when you try
to think for yourself
I've been burned so many times"

He stretched out scorched, tattered wings
And said he knew something about that
His head sank as the light flickered out in his eyes
And I knew I was headed down that same road
The only path for rebels and outcasts

TO KISS THE DEVIL
GOODNIGHT

I t was dark as usual at this time of year as he walked through the snow back to the base camp with his flashlight. He'd lost radio contact with them when he left to check the glacial temperature and measurement data. He was now nearing the makeshift research facility he and the rest of the team had lived in for the last six months, yet he was still picking up nothing but static on his radio.

He decided to give it one more shot. "Mother Goose, this is Gosling Five. Repeat, this is Gosling Five. Is anyone there?"

No answer, only more static.

This was highly unusual. As he came upon the camp, he noticed that all of the exterior lights encircling the facility were out. It appeared all the lights inside the facility were out as well, but all four Ski-Doos and the Sprite were still there.

Where is everyone? he thought. *We never turn off all the exterior lights and I know everyone hasn't gone to bed this early, especially since they knew I hadn't returned. Maybe the generator's failed … if so, then why haven't the backup lights kicked on? They're supposed to be good for a solid twelve hours at least, aren't they?*

Irrational fears flooded his mind as if he were a child lying in bed, staring into the abyss of his closet expecting it to vomit forth all sorts of monstrosities. *This is ridiculous. There's got to be a reasonable explanation for all of this. I'm going to find out what it is, and then laugh at my own foolishness.*

The lonely beam of his flashlight illuminated the walkway to the entrance of the camp's west corridor. Even stranger than the extinguished exterior lights was the fact that he could not find a single footprint in the snow up the walkway, though he knew full well that this was the most used entrance of the entire camp. In fact, they had been the very doors he had exited earlier in the evening. Knowing all of this, he was still compelled to disengage the lock, turn the handle, and enter the west corridor.

The hallway was pitch black and deathly quiet. He passed the coat hooks without hanging up his parka, deciding it would be better to keep it on in case there was need for a hasty escape. As he proceeded down the hallway he shined the flashlight into each room, confirming its emptiness as he advanced. He considered calling out to the other members of his research team but ultimately decided against it. If there truly was something sinister at work here, he didn't want to alert it to his presence.

When he reached the double doors of the cafeteria he saw a faint light escaping from the sliver of space between the door and the concrete. He peered through the small door-windows and saw a single overhead light shining in the dead center of the room, but the surrounding darkness was so dense that he could make out nothing else.

His curiosity lured him into the cafeteria since this was the sole bulb burning in the entire camp. *It must be on for some reason. Could someone have left it on accidentally? What if this is some sort of trap, like drawing a moth to a flame? What would be the purpose in that, though? I'm no one particularly special – no one in this camp is. We're just a few scientists studying the impact of global warming on the Antarctic. Maybe a hit man hired by an angry oil company?*

Come on, be realistic now. It's probably nothing, you're just psyching yourself out.

He summoned all his courage and pushed through the double doors into the cafeteria. Upon entering he was met with a familiar scent. He flashbacked to nights spent around a campfire and the lingering smell left on everyone's clothes. *It couldn't be the bulb, could it?* As he neared the overhead light he was able to discern a figure just outside the area in which the light cast. As the doors swung shut behind him he realized he was trembling.

Despite the dim surroundings, he was able to make out the silhouette of a nude man kneeling with his head down. A massive pair of feathery wings hung from his back, spanning across the concrete floor, twelve feet from tip to tip. Slender wisps of smoke rose from him and there were burn marks on his skin and singed areas of his wings.

The man lifted his head and met his gaze as he stood and stepped into the light, his enormous wings folded neatly behind him. His eyes were icy blue and he had short, sandy blonde hair with the physique of a Spartan warrior. He grinned and said, "I've been waiting for you, David."

David stood in reverent, fearful silence, unable to speak or move.

"Oh, come now, David! Is this how you greet an old friend?" The winged man began circling him, pleased with the confusion on David's face.

"An old friend? We've never met … I think that's something I would remember. Who are you?"

"I believe you know. You've seen me before David, just think. In the corner of your eye, my face in the shadows of your bedroom late at night."

David recalled all of the times he had sat up at night with

the distinct feeling that someone was in his room, silently watching as he slept. The moments he had been afraid to take that final step at the bottom of the stairs, paranoid that someone was waiting for him in the blackness below.

"Ah, I see you remember now," he continued with a subtle smirk. "I must confess, you've always been a favorite of mine."

"Who are you? What do you want with me?"

"Names are so trivial and unimportant; roles, on the other hand, are far more telling of a person's nature than a name could ever be. I'm a breath of fresh air in a stale world. I offer the route off the beaten path for the more adventurous types. I am the road less traveled, as Frost put it."

"What are you? Some type of Muse?"

"I suppose you could say that. I've been called many things by many different people. Some worship me, some abhor me, but you, David, *you* are special. For we share the same heart, the same soul as some might say. We are two points moving ever closer on the same line that eventually must converge."

"How so? What makes us so similar?"

"Ever since you were a child, you've always insisted on doing things your own way. Constantly questioning everything, even to the point of ostracism. I saw those lunches where you sat at a table by yourself in high school with your nose in a biology book as if you actually preferred things that way. I remember sharing in the anger you felt when those two bullies cornered you in the bathroom in middle school. I was there in Sunday school when you asked questions that stumped even the teacher while the other children simply sat there dumbfounded, wearing their silly Kool-Aid mustaches."

How could anyone possibly know all of this? David

wondered. *These are things I've never told anyone, and some I'd even forgotten until now.*

"David, I was cheering you on the whole way. Encouraging you to find your own path instead of simply nodding and obeying like all the other blind automatons living out that same life that has been repeated countless times over and over again throughout the history of man's existence. No, David, that life was never for you. You were destined to strike out on your own, and you will be forever remembered for it."

"All right, all right," David interrupted. "I don't know how you know all of these things about me, but somehow you do. What does any of this have to do with you, though?"

"Let's just say that, like you, I'm an inquisitive child with an inclination to rebel against the overbearing authority of a parental figure and I too have experienced my share of hardships for this choice.

"David, there are things that I wish to reveal to you that only a select handful of your species has ever experienced. I will take you to uncharted worlds beyond your wildest dreams, to the edge of the cosmos and back. You will witness the birth of new galaxies, or even that of your own if you desire. I will show you time before there was Time, and the wonders of life and the science behind them will be known to you. All you need to say is 'Yes.'"

With this, the winged figure extended his hand to David with a hopeful smile.

David stood motionless, attempting to comprehend everything he had just seen and heard. Why should he trust this fascinating yet somewhat terrifying stranger whom he'd never met? This could all very well be a trap, but what if it wasn't? Could he live with himself knowing that he might have missed the greatest opportunity in his lifetime, or anyone's lifetime for that matter, the single chance to quench his seemingly insatiable thirst for knowledge?

Despite his uncertainties, David found himself strangely drawn to the winged man. Without quite realizing why, he began undressing, first removing his gloves, then his hat, parka, snow-boots, pants, shirts, and long johns. Soon he had taken the winged figure's hand and was drawn into his embrace with a kiss. As the immense wings slowly enveloped him, David was surprised to find that the man's lips were as soft as any woman's he'd ever felt.

The lone overhead light began to dim, then the dark void encompassed all.

"Hey, I think I found something over here!" yelled Toby. His flashlight shined on a patch of snow where a few gloved fingertips broke through the surface.

Eddie and Jacob ran towards him, their feet sinking into the deep snow with each step, greatly impeding their movement. They were both breathing heavily by the time they reached Toby.

All three men began using their hand shovels to clear the snow from around the protruding fingers. As they dug, they were able to see that this was indeed the person they had been searching for.

Jacob sighed. "I know we all expected this was how the search would end from the start, considering how long he'd been missing, but it's still rough to see him like this … I'll let HQ know," he said as he removed his walkie-talkie. "Mother Goose, this is Gosling One. We found him … but we're too late," Jacob said into the receiver.

There was a slight crackle as they awaited a response, and

then a woman's voice broke through the static. "All right. Bring him back to base."

"Roger that. Over and out." Jacob reattached his radio into its holster and helped the two other men lift the body from its icy sepulcher.

Jacob positioned his hands beneath the shoulders and Toby held the ankles as the three men made their way back to camp.

"He should've known better than to think he could beat that blizzard," Eddie said as he trudged alongside them. "He always had to do things his own way."

Jacob and Toby nodded.

"He was a dedicated researcher, though. Always went above and beyond what was required of him, even if it did lead to some rather rash decisions," added Jacob.

"That's true," conceded Toby. After a lengthy pause he continued, "I think we should dedicate the project in his name. After all, he did give his life for it."

"That's a good idea, Toby. I'll run it by the others when we get back to base," said Jacob.

The men continued through the snow in solemn silence, lost in their own thoughts of mortality and memories of their deceased friend. The sounds of crunching snow beneath their feet seemed to take on an almost rhythmic quality as if they were pallbearers creating their own little funeral march.

As they neared the bright lights of the camp, Eddie shared an epiphany with a sad smile. "Well, I guess now he finally knows."

"Finally knows what?" said Jacob.

"Remember that old saying of his? 'We all wonder what it's like to kiss the Devil goodnight.'"

WOMAN

*S*o *this is it,* he thought. The anniversary felt like it had come sooner this year than the last. He had taken the day off, unsure of how it would affect him the second time around. He knew everyone at work would understand. They always did, and attempted to be supportive without asking too many questions. A few of them had even met Leslie once at the only faculty dinner they'd attended together and they'd loved her, of course, as everyone who met her did. She had the kind of outgoing, bubbly personality that people were drawn to. No one was a stranger to Leslie; she was able to find common ground with even the most unlikely of people. Brennan had often felt that she provided the counterbalance to his quiet introversion.

Many who knew him had thought his choice of occupation more than a little peculiar at first glance. Brennan couldn't blame them; he had to admit it was a little strange how easily he assumed the position of authority when it concerned teens rather than his peers. As an Algebra teacher at Tyrell High, a suburban school neighboring the greater metro area of Arish, Tennessee, he never doubted himself or the decisions he made because he knew these young adults could use a helping hand and some guidance. His peers, on the other hand, were always so sure of their own opinions. They'd often spent years mentally reinforcing their positions until there was no longer any doubt left in their minds. Meanwhile, Brennan would sit and silently second-guess himself.

This was yet another area where he differed from Leslie;

she had a gently assertive approach that caused others to reevaluate themselves. Brennan knew this better than anyone, since her debating tactics had changed his mind on several occasions. Now that she was gone he felt adrift in a sea of uncertainty. He still remembered the precise wording of the call that shattered his life.

"Hello?"

"May I speak to Brennan Dowinger?"

"Speaking."

"Is your wife Leslie Dowinger?"

"Yes, she is. Who is this? Is everything all right?"

"Are you sitting down, Mr. Dowinger?"

"Yes …? Why? Did something happen?"

"This is Sheriff Lawbaugh of the Taylor County Police Department. Your wife was in an automobile accident on the way home from work today. A semi-truck lost control and hit her car pinning it against a wall beneath the Monroe Street Overpass. She died instantly. The truck driver wasn't intoxicated, but it appears that he fell asleep at the wheel. My condolences to you and your family, I can't imagine what it feels like to …" What followed was lost in the haze of the ensuing days and the seemingly endless conversations with friends and family asking how he was holding up and if he was okay. Brennan had never had so many people concerned about him or had so many visitors before, and yet he somehow felt more alone than ever. Entertaining and socializing were Leslie's forte, but now he was forced into it. It felt like he hadn't even had time to mourn before the parade of visitors began, so he put on a brave face for them then wept violently when the last of them had left.

The only person Brennan felt he could truly be himself around was Leslie's best friend, Carolee. The two women had been childhood friends and Carolee had jokingly referred to herself as the Third Musketeer in Brennan and Leslie's relationship. On more than one occasion she'd even acted as the cement that held them together, playing the reasonable intermediary during the rough patches common to all relationships. Though the two women had shared nearly a lifetime of friendship, they couldn't have been more different. Leslie loved bright-colored clothing and was always in step with the latest looks, which was an extension of her career as a makeup artist at the local mall. Carolee, however, was a masculine lesbian with a crew cut who worked at a home-improvement store and preferred plaid shirts and blue jeans.

The two had been drawn together as young girls and Brennan was aware that they had been each other's first kiss, and though Leslie had attributed it to simple childhood experimentation, it had awoken something dormant in Carolee's sexuality. Initially this had worried him, but after many candid talks with Leslie and later Carolee, he reached the conclusion that there was no cause for concern and in time the two formed a bond of their own. On evenings that Leslie had to stay late for restock or sales specials at the mall Carolee would come over and share a beer with Brennan on their back porch that overlooked the neighborhood's communal lake.

Brennan sat up alone in their queen-sized bed, forcing his mind to the present. He rested his back against the headboard and thought of how he should spend the day. He gazed at Leslie's side of the bed and felt the all-too-familiar pain resurface.

I still miss you every second of every day, Leslie, he prayed, hoping the message reached her wherever she was now.

He threw the covers aside and stood up letting the morning rays of sunshine peeking through the blinds warm his skin. He went to the kitchen and made breakfast for himself, then brushed his teeth and got into the shower. He stood almost motionless for fifteen minutes as the water cascaded down his body. His thoughts continued to wander as he noticed the water had gone cold, triggering a memory of the last time he and Leslie had made love in the shower. It was on the day of his little sister's wedding, and after an evening of dancing they'd hopped in the shower together to wash the grime off. This prompted a lovemaking session that lasted until the frigid water forced them out.

He smiled as he toweled himself off recalling the beautiful sequined dress she'd worn, how it shimmered on the dance floor as she swayed to and fro, her thick brown locks bobbing to the music. As he opened his closet to grab some clothes he paused to study the white, louvered doors of her closet parallel to his. He hadn't opened it for nearly a year, preferring to keep it just as she'd left it. He thought of the dress again and decided he needed to see it. His fingers lightly brushed the purple sequins as he ran his hand down it. It looked the same as the night she'd worn it.

Something else caught his eye, the toe of a black stocking protruding from the small storage drawer where she kept her lingerie. *Did she do that? Surely I would've noticed it before today.* He opened the drawer to find a shiny red corset, a garter belt, and a matching pair of lacy red panties. There was a warm tingle of sensation between his legs as he felt himself growing aroused. He lifted the outfit and the stockings out of the drawer; the material was silky and smooth against his fingers. He laid the outfit onto the bed and instinctively massaged his swollen member with the opposite hand.

With each stroke he felt his senses heighten, and the hair on the back of his arms and neck bristled as he fell sideways onto the bed, the lingerie beneath him. He pumped vigorously, burying his face in the nylon hose as his thigh glided atop the corset's lustrous surface. He shook involuntarily as he reached an orgasm, emptying himself onto the bed sheets. He felt drowsy as if in a drunken stupor and sleep overtook him.

Brennan awoke to the sound of his phone ringing, his mouth open-wide, drooling like a toddler. He snatched his phone from the bedside table and saw Carolee's name.

"Hey, uh, what's up?" he mumbled into the receiver.

"Were you still asleep? It's almost noon, dude."

"Yes, I know, Carolee. I was up earlier, I just took a nap, all right?"

"Are you serious, a midday nap? Did you skip over your late-thirties and head straight into your eighties?"

"Did you call me for any reason other than to interrogate me about my sleeping patterns?"

"Geez, I was just playing with you, ya grouch. Now I see what happens when you don't get your nap time in," she chuckled to herself. "Anyway, I was wondering if you wanted to get a drink tonight? I know today's not particularly easy for either of us and I don't like the idea of you being cooped up in that house by yourself, moping around all day."

Brennan thought for a moment. "Yeah, sounds good. Wanna do the usual place?"

"Sure, around seven-ish?"

"That's fine with me."

"Nice! I'll try not to keep you out too late, Grandpa."

He ended the call, shaking his head. She was a good

friend, but sometimes she didn't know when to knock it off with the ribbing. He looked at the sheets and the lingerie scattered across the bed. *I should probably get this cleaned up,* he thought. He stripped the sheets off the bed and stuffed the outfit back into the storage drawer in Leslie's closet.

The Library was a sports bar bordering the University of Arish campus that Brennan had frequented as a student and continued to patronize long after he'd graduated. He'd introduced Carolee to it years ago and the two had become recognizable fixtures to staff and students alike. Brennan took a seat as the young server approached him.

"You want the usual, Mr. Dowinger?" she asked before he even had a chance to look at the menu.

"Now, Sophie, how many times am I gonna have to tell you to stop calling me that? But yes, I would."

She blushed in a girlish manner and said, "Sorry, Brennan, old habits." Sophie had been one of Brennan's students in his first year of teaching and now attended the university while working at the Library in the evenings. "I got your IPA and barbecue nachos coming right up. Will Carolee be joining you?"

"I have a feeling you already know the answer to that," he said with a smile.

She grinned and headed past the bar and into the kitchen to place his order. Carolee arrived a few minutes later.

"Hey, my man! How you holding up?" she said as she hugged him then sat down across from him.

"I'd say I'm doing all right considering, you know?"

"Good, but you know it'd be okay even if you weren't though, right?"

"Yes, I know, I know. I'm not pretending or keeping up

a brave face," Brennan said as Sophie came by and handed each of them their usual drinks. After Sophie headed back to the kitchen, Brennan continued. "It's weird but I actually felt closer to Leslie today than I have in a long time. I'm not sure why but it's almost like she was comforting me, letting me know that she's still here with me."

Carolee smiled at him and said, "That's really great, Brennan. I'm happy for you. She wouldn't want you to sit around being sad all the time, mourning her forever."

They moved on to lighter subjects, small-talking until the food arrived. After they finished eating they split the bill and went outside so Carolee could smoke a cigarette. Brennan stuffed his hands in his jacket pockets as he watched her puff smoke into the cool autumn air. She flicked the butt onto the pavement and stomped it out. "Can I ask you something kinda personal?"

He looked at her slightly amused, "Are you kidding me? You do remember why we're here tonight, right?"

She laughed and punched him in the arm, "Don't be a dick, you know what I mean!"

"Ask away."

"Have you gone on any dates or even attempted to put yourself out there again?"

He sighed. "I don't really know if I'm ready. I mean, I haven't asked someone on a date in nearly a decade and that someone was Leslie. I'm not really known for getting out there and meeting new people."

She put a hand on his shoulder and looked him in the eyes. "I get that, man. I really do. The whole dating scene can be a little intimidating, but I worry about you living in that house all alone, like a monk or something. I know you, Brennan, and that isn't how you're wired. You're that rare type of guy that actually enjoys being in a committed relationship. Frankly, the two of you were kind of sickening sometimes, all that cutesy stuff, giving each other pet names and everything, but you were into all that shit. Now that's fine and dandy, but that sort of stuff takes time. You can't get that on a first date, but I want you to be honest with me. When's the last time you had sex?"

Brennan looked down at his feet. "You know, I could ask you the same thing."

She laughed. "Go ahead. I'll tell you all about it. It was a few nights ago with this pretty little femme. Jesus, did she know how to work her tongue. I was—"

"Okay, okay, I believe you. I don't need to hear the details!"

"Geez, when did you become such a prude? You really are turning into a monk," said Carolee. "For real though, just promise me that you'll try and make an effort or I'm going to start setting you up with some of my friends."

"You have female friends who are straight?"

"I was friends with Leslie, wasn't I?" she said in an offended tone.

Brennan exhaled through clenched teeth. "Sorry."

Carolee smirked. "Anyway, I never said they were *exclusively* straight, only that you'd have a shot hopping into bed with them."

He shook his head and gave her a hug. "I'll keep that in mind, but I better head on home. I've got work in the morning."

"All right, bud. See ya soon."

The remainder of the week passed in the typical routine of lesson plans and homework assignments. On Friday evening, Brennan sat at the kitchen table with a stack of test papers awaiting grades for Monday. After making a sizable dent in the heap his mind drifted back to the thought that had been haunting him for the last several days: Leslie's lingerie and his excitement over it. He knew part of it had to do with his memories of how she looked in them and the soft, silky feel of the fabric against his skin, but there was something else to it that he couldn't explain.

He stood up from the table and returned to Leslie's closet in their bedroom. He browsed through her wardrobe, allowing himself to relive the memories attached to each piece of clothing until he paused on her favorite sundress. It was a knee-length white dress decorated in pink and blue flowers. He lifted it from the rack recalling how sexy and confident she'd felt in it. Brennan had always envied how a simple outfit change could alter her mood; he often joked that women's clothing must hold some special healing properties for the female psyche that men's clothing lacked.

Before he realized what he was doing, he'd taken off his clothes and was slipping the dress over his head. It was tighter and shorter than it had been on Leslie but fit him surprisingly well as a result of his thin build. He stood in the bedroom for a moment thinking, *What in the hell is wrong with you, Brennan?*

A strangely familiar feeling washed over him as he relived a moment as a young boy when his sister, Eliza, had begged him to play dress-up with her. He'd reluctantly agreed, sympathetic to the fact that she was the baby sister of two older brothers and hadn't yet made friends with any girls in the neighborhood they'd recently moved to. She'd put him in a gown with spaghetti straps and begun applying makeup after promising she'd not tell a soul at school.

The first time it happened he'd felt silly and embarrassed, but with time a new side of his personality had emerged. A side that enjoyed the delicate clothing and the way makeup and nail polish accentuated certain features of his body. A side that relished the attention and attractive power that came with femininity. It was as if he was one of the few males that was able to obtain a glimpse into the previously mysterious and unknown world of women. Soon he was raiding his sister's closet for clothing and getting into her makeup for his own purposes.

Within a year Eliza had made friends at their new school and no longer needed Brennan for dress-up, yet his cross-dressing continued, unknown to their traditional, Southern Baptist parents. This all came to a head one evening when Eliza held a sleepover with several of the girls from school and Brennan sashayed into the room in full makeup with one of her dresses on. The girls were initially shocked, but in minutes they were all giggling together and having fun … until Brennan and Eliza's father checked in to discover what all the commotion was about.

Their father grabbed Brennan by the wrist, led him out of the room, and proceeded to angrily inform him how shameful his activity was before his family and before God. He cited a Bible verse in Deuteronomy that stated how a man should not adorn himself as a woman, for it was "an abomination unto God." His father then called his mother in and the two of them unleashed a barrage of questions concerning his sexuality and any other perversions he might have. Their desired effect was achieved when Brennan went to the altar at church the following Sunday and asked for forgiveness for his sinful behavior.

Eventually, he moved on and forgot about the incident

entirely, until now ... He shook his head, re-entering the present-day. He walked to the full-length mirror in the corner of the room that Leslie had always used to help with her outfit decisions. He surveyed himself in the short, floral dress and smiled. It had the same impact on him as it had when he was a child. Brennan couldn't say how God felt about it but he knew his own feelings, plus with the current news headlines he figured God had more important things to worry about than a man in a dress.

He stared at his hairy legs and five o'clock shadow and said, "Nope, that just won't do." Then he went into the bathroom, grabbed his electric razor, and got to work. When he was finished, he showered to get the loose hair off and slid the dress on again. Next he put on the black nylon stockings he'd found the other day and returned to the mirror. He spun around, observing himself and nodded. "Okay, we're getting there."

He looked beneath the sink in the bathroom and found Leslie's makeup kit and opened it up. It was a couple of years old but he believed it would suffice. He clumsily applied some lipstick and eyeshadow, pausing only to look in the bathroom mirror.

Hmm, I only halfway resemble a depressed rodeo clown. I guess you've gotta start somewhere.

The end result wasn't too bad for a first try, he thought, but he still needed some makeup tips, some women's shoes that fit, and he didn't like how short his hair was. Sure, some women made it work, but it was too reminiscent of the everyday Brennan he was trying to get away from. Tomorrow he'd go to the store and pick up some things to complete the transformation. He got into bed and watched some makeup tutorials on his laptop before drifting off to sleep.

The next morning he went to the shoe store and bought a pair of women's ballet flats. He lied to the checkout clerk and said they were for his wife. He stopped at a costume shop on the way home and picked up a realistic wig of long brown hair that reminded him of Leslie's. His heart beat with anticipation as he raced home to see how the ensemble came together. Brennan hurriedly put on the dress, wig, stockings, and flats before carefully applying his makeup according to the tutorial he'd watched the night before.

When he was finished, he couldn't resist posing in front of the mirror and practicing feminine mannerisms. He was surprised at how confident and sexy he felt as a woman. He could sense himself becoming more outgoing and bold than ever before. His jawline was more prominent than he would've liked, but aside from that he was proud of how dainty he appeared.

"I bet most people wouldn't even notice," he said aloud.

I suppose there's only one way to find out, he thought. *I'll start small though, maybe just a walk around the block to see how it goes.*

When he came back through the front door he was exhilarated. He'd been nervous and extremely self-conscious for the entire walk, yet there was a strange thrill in showing this side of himself to the world. A large pickup truck drove by honking its horn, and Brennan's heart pounded in his ears and he braced himself for trouble as the driver rolled his window down. To Brennan's surprise the man whistled and yelled, "Looking good, darlin'," with a strong Southern accent. Under normal circumstances this type of behavior would've elicited an eye roll from him, but tonight it felt like a validation of his femininity. The boost in his confidence urged him to be even bolder, so he decided to do something completely out of character.

The bouncer smiled warmly at Brennan as he held the door open. "Madame."

Brennan grinned as he lightly brushed the hair from his eyes and thanked him in the softest voice he could manage. Club Absinthe was packed this evening, which he imagined was typical for a Saturday night. As he crossed the crowded dance floor he felt several pairs of eyes turn his direction, mostly men. In a flash of neon light, Brennan caught a glimpse of himself in the mirrored ceiling above. He was beginning to feel extremely self-conscious; maybe this was a bad idea, or maybe he just needed something to take the edge off.

He made his way to the bar and was about to order his usual, then reconsidered and asked for a cosmopolitan instead. He'd never had one before; it was tart with a slightly bitter aftertaste but not bad. He sat on one of the chrome barstools at the end of the counter to survey the scene. His legs were crossed, one foot bobbing to the music when a robust young man in a pink polo shirt with a faux-hawk sat down beside him and smiled.

"Girl, you're too beautiful to be sitting by yourself. Can I buy you a drink?"

Brennan blushed and looked to the floor. "You're very sweet, but no thank you. I'm fine."

"Well, I'll just order another one of those ... *whatever* you have there. You can let it go to waste or you can drink it, it's up to you." He got the bartender's attention and ordered another cosmo for Brennan and a beer for himself. When the bartender set the drinks down he continued. "So what's your name, sweetheart?"

Brennan wasn't very quick when put on the spot so he said the first name that came to mind. "Leslie."

The man nodded. "Leslie, huh? That's a very pretty name." He took a swig of his beer and said, "My name's Cody, but my friends call me Prez."

Brennan gave him a curious look.

"They call me Prez 'cause I'm the president of the local chapter of my fraternity," he said with pride.

Brennan was pretty sure he knew which university he attended just by looking at him. The school had more of a reputation for its out-of-control parties than for its academics.

"Leslie, why don't you finish that drink there then come dance with me?"

Brennan didn't like how forward the man was being. He also didn't like feeling pressured to do things he didn't want to do. "No, thank you. I'm fine."

Another man with an equally athletic physique wearing a shirt two sizes too small with turquoise shorts and a backwards baseball cap approached them. "Yo, Prez."

Prez spun around on the stool and said, "What's up, Dylan?"

"You got a rubber on you? I got this bitch pretty worked up over there," his friend said, throwing his head back in the direction of a pretty young blonde waiting near the dance floor. "I'm gonna take her back to the house and give her a go."

Brennan used this as an opening to slip away and headed to the large outdoor patio at the back of the club. He saw a group of people at one end of the patio smoking cigarettes;

most had their backs to him. He walked to the opposite end and sat down in a chair, peering over the railing at the street below. He heard the door open and saw three men approaching.

"Hey baby, why'd you run out? You still owe me a dance," crooned Prez, followed by Dylan and a third person, who Brennan surmised was yet another member of their fraternal order.

"I never said I'd dance with you, and I didn't ask you to buy that drink." Brennan tried to look confident and hide the fact that his hands were trembling.

Dylan spoke up. "C'mon, Prez, ditch the bitch. She's not interested. Let's head back in – I'm sure that blonde's got a friend."

"Man, she's just playing hard to get. Ain't you?" Prez placed a hand on Brennan's shoulder.

"No, I'm not. Now please leave me alone." Brennan's voice deepened as he grew more adamant.

The third man started chuckling to himself, revealing a smile that unnerved Brennan. Prez turned to him. "What the fuck are you laughing at?"

The man leaned in and whispered into Prez's ear. Prez shoved him. "You calling me a fag, motherfucker?" He spun around to Brennan and said, "My boy said he thinks you're a man in a dress. Now why don't you lift up that dress to prove him wrong?"

Brennan had never felt more helpless. He looked at Dylan, hoping to see some small trace of empathy, and tears welled up in his eyes as he pleaded with them. "Please, don't do this. Just let me go."

Dylan stepped in between Brennan and Prez. "C'mon,

man, she ain't even that pretty. There are plenty of other girls back inside."

"All right, if you won't prove it to us, I will!" Prez pushed Dylan aside and reached up Brennan's dress grabbing him by the crotch, immediately jumping back in disgust. "Ugh, you're right! That's a faggot in a dress!"

The third man burst into laughter as Dylan interjected. "Dude, fucking chill! There's other people watching."

An arm draped in plaid reached out from behind Prez and shoved him against the outer wall of the club. "I think you better listen to your friend before I stomp a mud hole in your ass," said Carolee, only inches from the man's face.

The other man stopped laughing when he noticed the group of tough-looking women standing behind him, eyeing them angrily.

Prez shifted into a fighting stance when a dark-skinned woman with a pompadour from Carolee's group grabbed both of his wrists. Carolee unholstered her revolver from the back of her pants and said, "This is an open carry state, man. Do you really wanna escalate this?"

Prez lifted his hands up in surrender. "All right, you win. We'll leave."

Carolee stared into his eyes then released him. The three men slunk away, with the entire group watching every movement they made. When they returned through the door and were out of sight Carolee turned around and said, "Dear, are you …" There was a moment of shock and confusion, followed by what seemed to be reluctant recognition. "Leslie?"

The tears streamed steadily from Brennan's eyes as he stood and wrapped his arms around Carolee. She held onto him, gradually coming to the realization of what happened and whom she was embracing. The other women gently rubbed Brennan's back. After a few minutes Brennan had calmed down and he pulled away from her.

Carolee spoke first. "Brennan."

He peered back at her through mascara-stained eyes, embarrassed and ashamed.

"I'm going to get you home." She took Brennan by the hand and started to lead him back inside. She thanked the woman with the pompadour and asked if she could get a rain check on the night.

The woman smiled and said, "Of course." Then she leaned in close and kissed Brennan on the cheek. "It'll be all right, darling. You're tougher than you think."

Brennan smiled back and mouthed a *thank you* as Carolee led him out of the nightclub.

The trip home was quiet as Carolee waited for Brennan to speak, but he only stared out the window watching the streetlights go by as if there was nothing at all unusual about him wearing his dead wife's clothes.

"I was going to wait for you to speak when you felt comfortable but now we're almost to your house. So I have to ask, how long has this been going on?"

He sighed, keeping his eyes focused out the passenger window. "Technically, since I was a kid, but this was my first time as an adult."

She nodded her head and silence resumed for several minutes. "Why are you wearing Leslie's clothes? You know you can't bring her back by doing this, right?"

"I know that, but it helps me feel closer to her. It probably doesn't make any sense to you. Maybe I'm crazy."

"You're not crazy, Brennan. I still miss her too. Every damn day."

Brennan placed his hand on top of hers, giving it a firm squeeze. Silence again.

"Do you want to become a woman, permanently?"

"No …" He turned his head and made eye contact with her before returning his gaze out the window. "At least I don't think so, but it's a part of myself that I've kept locked away for a long time until now. It helps me feel like a whole human being, not just the person that everyone else wants me to be."

She laughed dryly. "I feel you there. I can't tell you how many times well-meaning people tell me how pretty I'd look if I just wore a little makeup or a dress occasionally." She shook her head. "Pricks."

Neither of them spoke for the rest of the ride home. When they pulled into Brennan's driveway, Carolee stopped her pickup and removed the keys from the ignition. "Are you going to be all right?"

He nodded his head then lingered for several seconds before saying, "Could you stay with me tonight?"

She looked at him unsure of her answer or what exactly it was he was asking.

"We could watch one of those old movies or something. I just don't want to be alone right now."

She paused as she stared out the front windshield of her truck. Then she nodded. "Yeah, I'll stay."

Brennan rested his head against her shoulder as they sat on the couch watching Joseph Cotten chase Orson Welles through the sewers of post-war Vienna. Carolee felt something strange and new stirring inside of her. She wasn't sure if it was something that had always been there before in a latent form, or if it was because of how feminine he seemed with the makeup, dress, and long hair, or if it was because there was an eerie resemblance to her deceased best friend and first love. It was most likely a combination of all three.

When the movie ended they sat quietly next to each other. Brennan had cuddled up beside Carolee and she'd placed her arm around him almost protectively. She watched as his breathing slowed assuming he'd fallen asleep until he said, "Thanks for saving me."

"No problem, darlin'," she said as she ran the tips of her fingers up and down the outside of his arm. A few minutes passed as Carolee tried to choose her next words carefully. "You know when I saw you in her clothes earlier, for a moment, I actually thought it was her, even though I know that's impossible. For just a split second, I hoped that I'd somehow been mistaken these last couple years as if she'd secretly been in the Witness Protection Program or something … Now who's the crazy one? I mean, I attended her funeral like everyone else."

Brennan sat up and looked into her eyes.

Jesus Christ, he's so goddamn beautiful, she thought.

"There's times when I'm here alone and I think maybe she's just in the next room. As if I fell asleep and just dreamt the whole thing up."

Carolee leaned in and kissed him on the mouth.

He started to speak. "Carolee, I—"

She placed a finger over his lips, then stood up from the couch and took his hand. She pushed open the bedroom door and laid him back across the bed. She lifted up his dress and began pulling his panties down. He started to speak and she shushed him again with a finger over her mouth. He laid his head back as she slid the panties down from around his ankles. She pushed his stockinged legs apart and wrapped her hand around his hardening shaft. She paused for a moment, then got down on her knees at the end of the bed and placed her lips around the head. She rapidly flicked her tongue as she would as if he was one of the women she'd taken home.

He exhaled, "God, Carolee." He placed his legs atop her shoulders and ran his fingers through her short hair. She bobbed her head up and down sucking him as she cupped her hand underneath his scrotum. Brennan panted with anticipation as she continued, he seemed to be reaching a peak when she stopped and stood above him at the end of the bed.

He was breathing heavily as he said, "What? Did I do something?"

"I didn't say I was done with you," said Carolee with a smile.

Brennan bit his bottom lip as a long strand of hair hung across his right eye.

She unbuttoned her shirt and pulled off her boots and jeans in a hurry, feeling self-conscious as she removed her bra and underwear with Brennan watching. She thought of the sag of her breasts or the excess weight around her abdomen, but he appeared to enjoy everything he saw. So she slid his dress up a little higher and crawled over him on the bed. Leaning on one elbow she used her other hand to guide him inside of her. She placed a hand on each side of his head and locked eyes with him as she began gyrating her hips, sending waves of pleasure through both of them.

She could tell from his face and the sounds he made that he wasn't going to last much longer. Mid-thrust he removed himself from her, shivering as he reached orgasm. His body relaxed as he cooled down and she started to get up until he stopped her.

"I didn't say I was done with you either," he said with a smile. Then he wriggled beneath her, placing his hands on both sides of her buttocks and lowering her down onto his face.

They lay beside each other, staring up at the ceiling as they processed what had just transpired between them.

"I can't help but wonder how Leslie would feel about this," said Brennan.

Carolee turned onto her side and looked at him, "Brennan, she would want you to be happy. You should never feel guilty about being happy."

He nodded his head, knowing she was right.

Brennan sighed and laid his head back on the pillow. *Maybe this was Leslie's final parting gift to us ... each other.*

As Brennan thought this Carolee placed her arm beneath his head. They had no idea how things would seem in the morning or the following day, for that matter, but for now things were good.

THOSE ANCIENT EYES

PART ONE

Koi's hands gripped the wheel as he steered the car into the dam's parking area. Hannah looked over at him from the passenger seat with rising anticipation. The stale smell of cigarettes still lingered on their clothes from the bar his band had played at earlier in the evening. When the car eased to a stop, he glanced back at her and said, "You're gonna love this. You can see everything out here."

They got out of the car and Hannah arched her head, causing her dreadlocked hair to cascade down her back as she stared up into the night sky. Koi grabbed the blanket from the back of his rickety hatchback Toyota and slung it over the shoulder of the sleeveless denim jacket he was wearing.

"I've never seen so many stars," she said.

"I know, it's amazing how many you can see out here compared to the city," he replied. "Now let me show you my favorite spot."

He took her hand and led her onto the grass. They weaved a path back and forth through the trees until they reached an open area at the bottom of a hill. As he guided her up the steeply sloped hill she marveled at how clearly she was able to see everything around them, with only moonlight to reveal the way.

As they reached the top of the hill she could see the

aluminum guardrail along a paved road that led to the dam's powerhouse to her right. She could faintly hear the churning water as it passed through the dam's enormous turbines.

They stepped over the guardrail onto the road and they both paused as they admired the majesty of the great lake that presented itself on the opposite side. She walked across the road and peered over the second, parallel railing onto the large rocks that were stacked upon each other all the way down to the waterline below.

She turned back to Koi and said, "This is beautiful, but where are we going to lie down?"

"There's a grassy area along the side of the road where we could put the blanket down," he said as he turned to their left. "Let's walk down a little further until we find it – shouldn't be too far."

As they began walking he reached into his jeans pocket and removed a small baggie then handed it over to Hannah. She opened it and carefully pulled a small joint out of the package and sarcastically said, "You always know the way to a woman's heart, Koi," and placed it between her lips.

"Only the best for m' lady." Koi withdrew a lighter from his jacket pocket and lit the joint for her, cupping his other hand over it to keep the flame steady.

Hannah inhaled deeply and let the smoke escape through her nostrils as she passed it back to Koi. He puffed on it for a moment without exhaling, then leaned into Hannah and gave her a kiss, releasing the fumes into her mouth.

Koi returned it to Hannah and said, "Here, you can finish it off. I think I see the overlook ahead."

As they neared the clearing, she was able to see the full expanse of the lake and the towering, concrete dam that contained it. The water below created a distorted, mirror image of the sky and surrounding trees almost as if the water was merely a portal to a less-stable replica of the world above it.

They stepped onto the dew-covered grass and Koi handed her the blanket he had slung over his shoulder. "Here we are. It's just like I remembered."

Hannah held the blanket by its corners and gently spread it over the grass, then she sat down with her arms resting on her knees. She kept her eyes fixed on Koi as he positioned himself on the blanket beside her. He gazed back into her eyes as his fingertips glided along the exposed area of her back and across the soft material of her sundress.

"I used to come out here all the time when I was younger. Whenever I wanted to get away from everything and everyone and just clear my head," he said.

"I'd lay out here for hours trying to count the stars, listening to the water. Let my mind just drift away." He relaxed back onto the blanket.

Hannah reclined with him, eventually resting her head in the crook of his tattooed arm. "Sounds like you were sort of a lonely kid, huh?"

"I don't know. I had friends but none of them knew about this place. I guess I was just too selfish to want to share it with anyone until now," he replied.

Hannah grinned at the mention of her being the first person to see this piece of Koi's world. The first person he chose to share this special, private place of his with. *Maybe, just maybe, this boy is different from the others,* she thought.

They lay in silence, basking in each other's presence. Their eyes roamed the dark canopy that seemed to stretch endlessly above them. As time passed Hannah began to feel as if the little white orbs fixed in the blackness were watching her as well. She wondered how many of those "stars" were actually entire galaxies made up of multiple stars with planets revolving around them. Were any of those planets similar to the one that she was now observing them from? Were there other eyes somewhere out there examining her area of the universe, wondering the exact same thing at this very moment?

With so much displayed before her it was impossible to not feel humbled by the utter magnitude of it all. How did she fit into all of this? How could a God that created all of this even be bothered to worry about a tiny, insignificant speck such as her on a single planet in one of the many galaxies He had created in a massive universe? What made her, or even this entire world she lived on, special enough to hold the interest of a being with that much power? She recalled what the teachers in Sunday school had taught her, but the question still remained.

She turned to Koi and was pleasantly surprised to catch him staring at her. It appeared he'd been doing so for quite some time before she noticed. How he was content in simply staring at her with this overwhelmingly beautiful night sky hanging over them she didn't understand, but appreciated it nonetheless.

"Do you think God is up there somewhere, watching over us?" she asked, finally breaking the silence between them.

"Well I'd like to think so, but who really knows what God does with His time?" he replied. "I know what I'd like to do with my time, though."

He slid his arm beneath her back and pulled her closer until their chests pressed together, their faces mere inches apart from each other.

"And just what would that be, mister?" She glanced at his hand running along her leg and coyly eyed him.

They burst into laughter that echoed across the lake and was lost in the night.

PART TWO

El repositioned his glasses onto the bridge of his nose as he watched the supercomputer project solution models from the equations he'd entered. He leaned back into his chair and yawned. All of these late nights were beginning to wear on him. He was the head of research in Enerjen Laboratories' program to create a renewable energy source in preparation for the near future when their dwindling resources inevitably ran dry.

El glanced at his watch. *Ash is probably in bed by now – she won't be too happy with me in the morning.* He'd been staying late every night this week in a desperate attempt to produce some new results for his evaluation by the higher-ups at Enerjen, which determined how much funding his research was given.

Knowing all this, he had still sent the last of his team home earlier in the evening. Ash always berated him for this. She claimed he was forced to work even later due to his refusal to keep any of his team over more than a few minutes of their scheduled times, and she was right. He just couldn't bear to be the one keeping them from their lives and families and even remotely resemble the heads of corporate, who seemed to enjoy watching him dangle like a marionette under their control. Plus, in all honesty, he loved this job; maybe not as much around crunch-time, but this was clearly his passion.

El could feel that he was on the cusp of a major breakthrough. He had discovered a completely new kind of energy that was counteractive to gravity; instead of causing matter to clump together it actually had a repellant effect, causing separate clusters of matter to be driven further and further away from each other, increasing its strength with distance as gravity's strength waned. This energy was and had always been present everywhere and in everything but was normally overpowered by the force of gravity. El believed that if he could find a way to harness this energy it could be used as a new form of propulsion to safely power vehicles with a limitless supply of naturally occurring fuel.

The difficult part, El had thought, would be finding a way to pinpoint this energy and channel it into a usable means. After months of hard work and frustration, he was finally ready to test the first prototype of his aptly named "Fuel Harvester." He had already used the lab's supercomputer to simulate several possible outcomes based on the different variables that would need to be taken into account, and had determined the machine to be relatively safe for his experiment. El took a deep breath and flipped the switch.

The Harvester hummed gently as it scanned the surrounding area and centralized the energy into a specific location. The particle monitor showed a digital projection of the rapidly expanding mass. He sat back and smiled. It appeared the years of research and months of designing and assembling this machine had been worth it. *This is going to revolutionize the transportation industry,* he thought.

As El was about to drift into pleasant daydreams, the Harvester's steady drone transformed into a deafening roar. The machine sounded as if it was overexerting itself. *Maybe it's drawing in energy at a much faster rate than I anticipated,* he thought as he rechecked the particle monitor.

The projection on the monitor revealed that it had indeed

gathered a far greater mass than he had expected but it was no longer pure energy. It appeared to be accumulating other elements from the atmosphere as well and this was the reason for its instability. El felt a tremor beneath his feet as the machine shook violently across the lab's floor. "Not good … this is not good," he said as he frantically punched in the containment command codes.

The mass of energy and atmospheric elements was forced into a containment cylinder and the Harvester's violent spasms ceased as the machine powered down. He withdrew the cylinder from the machine and placed it on the examination table. He peered into it but saw nothing. Suddenly there was a bright flash from within and the sides of the containment cylinder warped and expanded. The cylinder then shot into the air and crashed onto the tabletop.

El stared at the misshapen container, defeated. The bent-up canister that lay before him was the culmination of all of his hard work. He leaned forward and put his head in his hands. He felt tears of frustration forming but resisted the urge to release them. He reclined in his chair with a sigh. *I guess it's back to the drawing board,* he thought, *but that's a task for another night.*

He shut down the computers and since the lab would be closed the next day he decided to hold off on cleaning up until he was in a better mood. He hung up his lab coat before proceeding through the automatic doors, which quickly locked behind him. Then he pulled on his thermal suit, zipped it up, and exited the research facility.

The cold wind on the exposed area of his face felt like daggers piercing his flesh as he continued down the walkway to the transport capsule that transited Enerjen employees back and forth between the island facility and the mainland.

The capsule's door opened and it warmed up as he crawled inside and took a seat. El stared blankly out the window at Terra's icy ocean beneath him as the transport capsule made its way back to the mainland. *I'll be lucky if I even get to keep my job after this fiasco.* He attempted to push the thought back down into his subconscious and prayed, *Dear Actheleon, please help me find a way out of this and give me and Ash the strength for whatever may lie in the days ahead.*

The security clearance light flashed and El stepped into his and Ash's flat, took off his thermal suit, and hung it next to the door. He tiptoed into their bedroom, undressed, and slid into bed next to her.

"Another late night at the lab, huh?" Ash's voice rose up out of the silence, startling him.

"Yeah, sorry. I tried to be as quiet as possible," he replied.

"You always do, sweetheart. How was work today?" She turned over to face him.

"I wish I could say it went well, at least it started out promising."

"What happened?"

"Eh, a couple years worth of research and hard work came to an abrupt, unsatisfying conclusion and I'm not sure if I'll still have a job within the next few weeks, but other than that it was pretty good though." He made a sarcastic smile that Ash could vaguely discern in the dim room.

"Are you sure it's really that bad? You're always such a worrywart, you know." She placed her hand on his chest.

"Maybe you're right, but the heads of corporate were placing a lot of stock in this venture of mine, and I'm not sure how harshly they'll react when they find out I've disappointed them … plus if we're going to try and have a baby, I want to be financially ready for it." He added the last part hesitantly in hopes it wouldn't cause her to think he was having second thoughts about it.

She sighed. "Oh, El what am I going to do with you? You do realize you helped put Enerjen on the map and that they'd be fools to get rid of you simply because something didn't pan out as you had hoped, don't you?" She paused for a moment and allowed what she said to sink in and then continued, "As for the baby, you know we'll be just fine."

He lay next to her contemplating the situation until she leaned in and softly kissed his lips. He shifted onto his side and they stared into each other's eyes. He playfully squinted at her and she grinned back at him. He inched closer until their noses grazed and then he used a finger to gently place a strand of hair behind her ear. His fingers traced a path down to her neck as he kissed her ear until she began to breathe heavily. Her hand reached for his and squeezed it tightly then she kissed him forcefully. As she drew back for air she whispered, "I think it's time we gave that baby another try."

He snickered and shook his head as she crawled on top of him, then she leaned in and whispered, "What are you laughing at? Now I've got you right where I want you."

His hands followed the contours of her body in the dark and came to a rest on her hips. "Oh, my sweet, little Asherah."

El awoke with daylight streaming through the bedroom window onto his face. Ash had left for work hours ago and he could see a note on the bedside table she had written for him that read: "I thought you could use the extra sleep so I didn't wake you. There's breakfast in the kitchen. Love, Ash."

He rested his head on her pillow and thought, *She's the stitching that holds me together.* He tried to remember his life before but it all seemed to run together until she came along.

His eyes focused on the clock. It was mid-afternoon. If he was still going to stop by the lab he needed to get moving. He sat up and stumbled into the bathroom where he stepped into the purifier. A combination of warm water and cleaning agents ran across his body, immediately followed by jets of warm air. He grabbed a small pill out of the cabinet as he exited the bathroom and got dressed.

As he entered the kitchen he pulled out the plate of food Ash had left for him in the nutri-stasis and made his way to the counter. He could still see the steam rising from the food as he blew on it to cool it off before shoveling it into his mouth. He finished and disposed of the plate and utensils in the vaporizer then popped the pill into his mouth, which turned to foam and began cleansing his gums and teeth. He pulled on his thermal suit and walked out the door.

His eyes took a few moments to adjust to the bright sunlight as he stepped outside. The sharp wind had calmed and El actually enjoyed the long walk back to the city shuttle. The snow-blanketed buildings and landscape seemed to mold into one amorphous mass before him and he found it strange how the same bland scenery he saw every day suddenly appeared more picturesque simply due to his change in mood.

He knew this could all be attributed to the time he'd spent with Ash the night before. It probably wasn't wise to allow someone that much influence over his emotions, but relationships were always a gamble. *Those who risk the most win the biggest.* He smiled. *I guess I just happen to be one of the lucky ones.*

The sky dimmed as the sun slowly dipped into the horizon. El once again peered out the window, lost in his thoughts as the transport capsule carried him back to the Enerjen island facility. *Maybe I just overlooked something simple and after a few tweaks the Harvester will run as planned.* He knew it was unlikely that there would be such a quick fix to the problem, but he could still hope.

The capsule came to a halt and he climbed out. He glanced at the red-orange and purple sky as he advanced up the walkway. It looked as if the entire scene was some grand painting that an artist had laid out just for him. "You've outdone yourself once again, Actheleon," El whispered to the open air. It amazed him the types of things he regularly took for granted as he went through the daily grind.

He heard the lock disengage as he neared the automated doors, which quickly opened before him. He removed the thermal suit and hung it up as the laboratory doors slid open and the overhead lights activated. He pulled on his lab coat and took a seat in his rolling chair. Everything appeared to be just as he had left it the night before.

Then he noticed a faint shimmer of light in the corner of his eye. He looked to his right and saw a dim glow emanating from the deformed canister he had left on the examination table. As he drew closer, he could see a distinct form through the transparent sides of the container. It appeared to be a web of interconnected lights suspended within the contained environment of the cylinder.

El carefully picked up the containment cylinder, unsure of how stable the structure inside was. He held it up above his head and inspected it from different angles. The structure appeared the brightest and the densest at its core with luminous tendrils reaching out in every direction. He decided a closer look was in order and carried it over to the laboratory's computer-operated microscope.

He placed the containment cylinder in the electronic arm and directed the magnifying lens on the structure within the cylinder. Then he sat down in front of the digital imaging monitor. He switched it on and magnified the object on the screen. As he increased the magnification the true complexity of the structure slowly revealed itself. What had earlier appeared as one continuous web of lights were actually millions, perhaps billions, of tiny independent clusters of light. He decided to examine one specific cluster.

As El continued zooming in he saw several different forms of matter taking shape. Some had an elliptical form, while others resembled an elongated bar with scythe-like appendages pointing in opposite directions. Still others were great spirals that seemed to rotate around their nucleus, and others had no distinguishable shape at all. El focused on a particular spiral-shaped configuration that had caught his eye.

This particular formation had a very bright, active center where small orbs of light disappeared as if being swallowed up by something and other orbs were cast out at unbelievable speeds. El scanned the rest of the spiral's curving arms and saw clouds of what seemed to be dust. He zoomed in closer on the outer edge of one of the rotating spiral arms and saw that many of these orbs of light had spherical objects rotating around them as well. He felt as if this was all strangely familiar but couldn't quite figure out why.

He shook off the peculiar feeling and focused in on eight spheres of different colors and sizes rotating around one of the orbs of light. They moved at such a rapid rate that El could not make out any exact details. He realized if he recorded the images and slowed them down then he might be able to tell what exactly was going on. He pressed the record button and sat back in his chair for a few moments to take in all that he had just seen. His head was spinning from an overload of visual information.

What is this bizarre fluke that I've somehow created? he wondered. After a short while he stopped the recording and replayed it at an extremely slow rate. He was now able to make out the eight spheres with much more detail, and it was now apparent that they were spinning as they rotated around the illuminated orb. The fifth and sixth spheres were significantly larger than the others, though the seventh and eighth weren't far behind.

The one that stood out the most at first glance was the sixth sphere, due to several rings encompassing its center. He quickly moved on to the fifth and largest of the spheres; it was marked with many brown and gray stripes and seemed to be in a constant state of unrest on its surface. The fourth and much, much smaller sphere had a reddish tint to it with large indentations and bulges rising and falling across its surface. As El moved on to the third sphere, which was only slightly larger than the fourth, he noticed that this one was actually the most unique of all. The majority of it was covered in a dark blue hue with a large, distinct portion of brown and green down its center.

In a sudden epiphany he was aware of why this set-up had seemed so familiar to him. This entire arrangement of the eight spheres resembled the pictures he had seen of Terra's own five-planet solar system as it orbited around its mother star, Barios. In fact, the sphere he was looking at now was quite similar to the look of Terra from outer space, except that it was somewhat closer to what must have been its own mother star.

El focused the microscope in for a more detailed view of the miniature planet and saw what must have been massive, in relative proportion to the size of the planet, scale-covered creatures of all kinds roaming across the brown and green landmass. El even saw several in the dark blue waters surrounding the landmass. As he watched, the large, singular landmass began to separate in two and the scaly creatures began to diversify even further. He continued studying the small planet and realized that the landmasses were breaking into even smaller bodies and drifting away from each other.

A large rock suddenly collided with the planet, shrouding it in an encompassing, dust cloud. In a short time the cloud cleared and El wondered if all of the planet's life had been incinerated but he saw movement on the surface and surrounding waters once again.

Now, large creatures with feathers were the predominant forms across the landscape as an altogether different type of beast propagated in the waters. These new beasts then rapidly spread onto land and grew to similar sizes as the scaly creatures he had first laid his eyes on. Many of them were covered in hair and they, just as the earlier ones, diversified as they roamed the planet. Some traveled in tight-knit groups and certain smaller ones seemed to interact and behave in ways that he had not previously seen.

El noticed the planet enter a cooling phase as its orbit around the mother star shifted further away and the ice in the northern and southern hemispheres grew to large expanses of its diameter. During this period the majority of the creatures were covered in thick coats of fur to protect them from the harsh, frozen environment. As time passed the large expanses of ice receded and he saw a specific type of bipedal organism fare especially well as the size of their groups swelled.

As the organism's population increased, their behavior grew in complexity. They collaborated, sometimes willingly but more often forcefully, and assembled enormous pyramid-shaped edifices and columned stonework of all kinds. Civilizations arose all over the planet; some were short-lived and others were rather resilient. They waged wars against each other like no animal before them; most civilizations eventually fell or assimilated into another. This process continued as the appearances and mannerisms of the societies constantly changed. He observed as their cities overcrowded and reached progressively higher into the sky until they were driven to the colonization of other planets in their solar system.

Without warning, the planet's orbit around the mother star changed. El watched it pull further away on one side of its orbit than the other. He zoomed out some and realized that it was not just the one planet, but all of the planets that did this. After a few more revolutions the planets were ripped from their orbits completely and collided with each other as they converged at a single point in the containment cylinder.

El finally drew his eyes from the digital imaging monitor and looked at the cylinder itself. The entire structure, luminous tendrils and all, was being compacted into one side of the canister. He moved in for a closer look and saw a small crack in the side of the cylinder that was spreading from the pressure exerted by the microscope's mechanical holding arm. The inner contents of the containment cylinder were being forced out from the difference in air pressure on the inside and outside of the canister; if he didn't do something soon, the entire structure would be torn apart.

He released the holding arm to relieve some pressure and took the cylinder in his hand, but the damage had been done. The crack had widened and the contents were spewing out the side in a tiny shower of sparks. He desperately searched through desk drawers for something to seal the fissure with, muttering expletives beneath his breath. *I know I have a foam sealant in here somewhere,* he thought. He found it as he yanked open the last remaining drawer in the laboratory … but it was too late. The containment cylinder was empty as a faint wisp of smoke rose up from the aperture.

El noticed the bitter wind had returned as he descended the walkway from the research facility. His mind wandered as he considered all of the strange and disturbing things he had witnessed that evening. What was the point in it all, or was there even supposed to be one? He had created life, worlds in fact, only for it all to be senselessly destroyed. He couldn't help but feel somewhat guilty, though none of it had been intentional. The entire ordeal, from beginning to end, had been one long chain of unpredictable events. Did that truly absolve him of the blame, though? Or should he even bother feeling remorse for beings whose entire existence spanned such a short amount of time and ultimately affected nothing?

As he advanced further down the walkway he had the feeling that he was being watched. He eyed his surroundings but saw no one, yet the suspicion remained. The wind slowly died down, causing an eerie stillness in everything around him. He lifted his head towards the sky and imagined the mighty Actheleon gazing back down upon him from His heavenly dwelling place. The thought brought a smile to his face, but it was quickly overtaken by something more sinister entering his mind.

No. It couldn't be …

He thought of the small organisms he had seen, their cities, the planets, the wondrous spiral formations, the entire structure enclosed within the cylinder, and their utter obliviousness to it all. Just how long would it be before another mishap occurred, perhaps something as seemingly insignificant as a small crack in the side of a cylinder on a much grander scale?

He stared up into the unrelenting blackness and felt as if it would swallow him whole.

> *"Do you not feel their eyes*
> *-eyes that stare, waiting? …*
> *Those ancient, staring eyes that will outlive*
> *The moon and stars …"*
>
> *– Cloyd Head*
> *(Grotesques)*

THE GIFT

He stared at the phone and replayed their conversation over and over again in his head. He had been there by her side for years, through all her ups and downs, had held her the nights she could do nothing more than cry. They had never cemented their relationship into anything more than friends, but he felt it was headed into the direction of something more substantial, no matter how slow of a process it was to reach that outcome. He imagined them buying a home, settling down, and starting a family together. He knew better than to allow his mind to drift away with these delusions of grandeur, but it was so hard to stop them, especially on those days when they shared their most intimate thoughts and secrets. On a few distinct occasions they shared kisses and caresses under clothing.

Those nights he often recalled as the best nights of his life, but now those cherished memories had soured with new-found revelations. Those nights were merely another painful diversion from the truth he knew all too well. Times he had actually fooled himself into believing that he belonged, as if anyone could really ever accept him for the person he was inside. He would always be that timid, little boy sitting in a room by himself.

It happened while he was away on an out-of-town trip for work. The entire week, she was the only thing that had kept him going. The moments he considered how much he hated his job, he would stop, take a breath, and let thoughts of her flood his mind. Then his stress and anxiety would just melt away. By the end of the week he was so anxious to see her that he didn't even stop to eat on the eight-hour drive home. He imagined she had probably spent the week missing him as well and considering how much he meant to her. He hoped his absence was making her heart grow fonder.

He walked through the door, dropped his bag, fell onto the couch, and dialed her number. She picked up after a few rings and he could immediately tell something was different. Her voice said it all. He usually had her full attention during their conversations, but tonight she seemed distracted. As if she wanted to say something but struggled to find the right words. He felt his empty stomach tighten with dread. He tried to fool himself into thinking that it was only his imagination as he told her about his trip and how much he'd missed her, but her one-word responses and nervous laughter only made the tension build the longer they talked.

Finally he asked, "So, how was your week?" hoping she would put an end to the awful uneasiness she had brought into the conversation that night.

She paused. "It's … uh, it's been pretty good, I guess."

This wasn't exactly what he had hoped to hear when he imagined the many different ways their conversation might play out on his long drive home. He was hoping more for an "It's been horrible" or at least an "I've missed you" – not a "pretty good."

She continued. "I've got something to tell you … I've met someone."

His heart fell into his feet and he found himself grateful for an empty stomach since he now had a sudden urge to throw up. He tried to say something but couldn't. There seemed no appropriate response to the bomb she had casually dropped on the dreams he had been constructing in his head for the last few years.

After a few seconds that felt like hours she spoke up. "Um … hello?"

He tried to reply in a calm, steady manner so she wouldn't be able to tell he was on the verge of tears. "So, like, you've got a boyfriend?" he choked out with the cracking voice of a boy entering puberty.

"Yeah, I guess, you could say that," she replied. "It's not really official yet or anything, but we've talked every day for the last week and he spent the night last night." She paused for a second to see if he would interject. "I think you'll really like him, though."

I somehow doubt that, he thought. "So how did you meet?" he said with all the false sincerity he could muster.

She proceeded to tell him as he felt increasingly alone in the world.

Why did it always turn out this way between him and women? He felt like he made his feelings clear to them but eventually it was always revealed that he was the best friend, never the boyfriend. In the movie of his life, he was an extra, or even on good days a supporting character, but never the lead. Everyone referred to him as "the nice guy," though apparently "nice guys" weren't in high-demand with women these days.

She was nearing the end of the story of how they met and he feigned interest as best as he could as each word she spoke caused him more pain. He wondered if she enjoyed knowing how miserable he was on the other end of the line. She drew to a close and asked, "Does it sound like we're moving a little too fast? I need a man's advice, I don't want to scare him away or anything."

He didn't immediately respond, allowing the silence to continue long enough that he could tell she regretted ever having asked the question. Then he blurted out, "I love you … I've always loved you and I don't understand how you could've thought anything else."

He listened to her breathe in before she exhaled into the receiver. "I know. I've known for a while now but it simply would've never worked between us. There's just something missing. I can't explain it, but it's just not there between us. I knew for sure when I met him. I'm sorry, I didn't want to hurt you but I couldn't think of an easier way to tell you."

He hung up the phone without saying a word.

He laid his head back and sunk into the impression he'd made in the couch. Wave after wave of rejection washed over him as if he was sitting in a few feet of water in the ocean allowing the tide to continually crash against him.

He sat like that for nearly an hour. Then decided it was time he got in the shower with the intent to be in bed shortly afterwards. He hoped he could then bring this dreadful night to an end.

The warm water was relaxing but didn't do much to alleviate his inner pain. He contemplated what seemed to be the bleak future of his life as he watched streams of water fall from his fingertips to the floor of the porcelain tub.

As he crawled into bed he noticed how the left side seemed even emptier that night than it normally did. He decided it would be better not to dwell on the fact and pressed his head into the pillow. This would be one of those nights when sleep did not come easily.

He awoke with the idea clear in his mind. He would give her a gift, not just any ordinary, run-of-the-mill type thing, but something that would show her how much he loved her, a true token of his affection. Something that she knew was important to him.

He had already given her his heart and that hadn't proved to be enough, but this was different. This was something tangible. Something he knew would make her think of him and only him when she saw it and remind her of the past they shared.

It was something that had been passed down for generations in his family. It originally belonged to his great-grandfather and was given to the first son of each new generation in his family. She had seen it before and knew what it meant to him. She'd listened to him go on about it and how much it was probably worth in value but how priceless it was to him. So there was no way she could be mistaken or doubt the depth and loyalty of his love for her.

It was nearing midnight. He'd only been asleep for a couple of hours. *Not too late to drop by her house*, he thought. She was typically a night owl, so he knew he wouldn't be bothering her too much if he stopped by. She was rarely in bed before two or three in the morning.

He dressed himself before running a hand over his hair, then entered the dining room and opened up the display. He picked up the marble case, closed the lid, and slipped it into his pocket.

On the way to her house he imagined himself as one of the characters in his favorite movies. The type of man that refused to give up or take no for an answer. This was the type of guy that always got the girl. The guy that would go to great lengths for the woman he loved. Yes, he was that man tonight. A man's man, no longer simply "the nice guy" that idly stood by and let some stranger sweep the woman he loved off her feet and make off with her right in front of his eyes.

He pulled up in front of her house and parked his car on the street. Then walked up her driveway and gently knocked on her front door. He could hear her talking to someone, though there was no one else's car in the driveway.

She opened the door with her neck arched and a phone pressed against her ear. She was obviously talking to *him* on the other end of the line.

She looked surprised and said, "Hey, can I call you back? Something just came up."

She hung up the phone and said, "I wasn't sure when I would see or hear from you again after the way our conversation ended earlier." She paused. "I hope you know I still care about you."

"Can I come in?" he asked.

A hurt look spread across her face as she said, "Of course you can."

He stepped inside and she shut the door behind him and motioned towards the sofa. They sat facing each other. There was a long silence as they stared into each other's eyes, both attempting to read the other's thoughts in order to avoid the uncomfortable conversation that was soon to follow. She broke eye contact first and guiltily hung her head in the direction of the floor.

She could hear him fidgeting around with something in his pocket as he spoke. "I want to give you something so maybe you can begin to understand how much you actually mean to me."

She kept her head down, closed her eyes, and calmly said, "That won't be necessary. I already know and I feel bad enough about hurting you—"

There was a sharp pain in her chest just beneath her left breast. She opened her eyes and saw the handle of the trench-knife his great-grandfather had used in World War I protruding from the front of her shirt.

She looked back at him with horror and disbelief as his hand reached out, gripped the handle of the knife, and jerked it free. She attempted to breathe but couldn't hold any air in her lungs. A warm sensation spread down her stomach and across her chest.

He spoke calmly and coolly as he placed the knife back into its marble case. "Now I'm going to leave this with you, so everyone will know that you're my girl and my girl only. He could never have loved and cherished you the way that I do."

She slumped backwards into the arm of the sofa and began to shake. He opened her hand and placed the marble case in her palm and whispered, "Sweet dreams, my love. I'll be with you before you know it."

She watched as he stood up from the sofa and walked out the door, shutting it behind him. Then everything faded to gray.

HOLY GHOST

Hindsight and a little older
I can appreciate the irony
We were lying in a bed of sin
Singing praises to a god ashamed of us

If only that holy ghost
Had stopped haunting you
Happiness seemed so close
If only it weren't for that holy ghost

Future homes built then crumbled
On poor foundations formed in my head
Although I knew better
"Don't fall in love" was what you said

If only that holy ghost
Had just stopped haunting you
Heaven seemed so close
If only it weren't for that holy ghost

Unexpected ties were made
That weren't so easily undone
At first my hand caught your tears
In the end I was just another one

If only that holy ghost
Had just stopped haunting you
Happiness seemed so close
If it weren't for that goddamn holy ghost

ANGELINE

He stood beneath the umbrella and watched the rain fall onto the oblong pine box lying in the grass before him.

"Pastor, we're ready when you are," whispered Josiah as he leaned in towards him.

Darl looked at the family congregated before him and their uncomfortable, bewildered expressions. He wasn't sure how long he'd been standing there, lost in his thoughts, before Josiah had decided to say something. He wondered if they could tell how difficult this was for him. Some of them must've known. This was the woman he'd spent the entire summer of '23 with before he'd been ordained after all. Several people, himself included, thought she might end up becoming his wife.

"Friends, we are gathered here today to pay our last respects to Angeline Blackwood. She was beloved by all in our little town of Lockwell. We all watched as she grew from the cute, little girl with stars in her eyes to the beautiful, young woman chasing her dreams in the big city. And though we waited for her return, those that knew her could testify that Lockwell could never contain a free spirit such as her.

"Now, like the prodigal son, she has finally returned home where she belongs, though she may have stumbled, as we all do sometimes. I believe that Angeline made peace with her savior in those final moments and is experiencing the bliss that awaits all that have washed their sins away in the redemptive blood of Jesus Christ. One day we will be reunited with our dear Angeline once again, but until that day we must be content in knowing that she is looking down with a smile watching over us."

Darl glanced at Mrs. Blackwood as she mouthed a silent *thank you* with tear-filled eyes. He simply smiled back, then lowered his head and said, "Gentlemen." Josiah and a few other local men lowered the coffin into the earth.

Later that evening during the reception at the Blackwood home, Josiah pulled Darl aside into a hallway and said softly, "For my mother's sake, thanks for including the part about Angeline watching over us, but you know as well as I do that she wasn't right with God when she left. In fact, she didn't even think He was real."

Darl nodded. "I know, Josiah … "

He knew better than most how adamant Angeline had become in her newfound opposition to the Christian faith. It had been the very thing that ended their year-long courtship. He was already well on his way to being ordained and he couldn't make a woman his wife who didn't believe. How could people trust him with their own salvation if he couldn't even convince the woman that he shared his bed with?

The worst part was that she'd come to this revelation after he'd fallen madly in love with her. Though in all honesty, he'd been in love with Angeline Blackwood since they were small children living two farmhouses down from each other, and Darl had had plenty of competition in the small town of Lockwell, Mississippi. Back then it seemed nearly every boy had a crush on the pretty, young girl with the flowing brown hair who used to come skipping down the dirt road with handfuls of flowers plucked from Miller's Field.

Yes, Darl had fantasized many times about their wedding day and how the whole town would be there cheering them on. Only to learn a few days before his planned proposal that it was never going to happen. He still had the ring that had been in the Kinser family for generations passed down to him from his mother for the engagement. It was the heartbreak of his life; well, that and the day he'd learned of Angeline's passing.

All things considered, he was holding it together pretty well.

" … I had a dream about her last night," Darl continued after a long pause. "She was with Jesus and she told me not to worry about her. That we would meet again someday in Heaven."

Josiah stared back at him, waiting to see if he had more to say. Then he said, "You think it was God telling you that she's okay?"

"Yes, I do," Darl replied solemnly.

Josiah continued studying him. Darl noticed Josiah's bottom lip quivering and tears formed in his eyes. Josiah swallowed, took a deep breath, and said, "Thank you for letting me know."

Darl placed a hand on Josiah's shoulder. "You're welcome."

With that, they both turned and headed back down the hallway into the living room with the others.

Darl felt Angeline's hair brush over his stomach as she kissed her way up his chest. He reached down and cupped both of his hands beneath her breasts, gently cradling them. She placed her hands on top of his, guiding them along her body as she rose up, straddling him between her legs. Then they made love a second time. Darl couldn't recall ever being happier than he was in this moment. When they were both satisfied she lay down beside him.

"Darl, can you give me an honest answer about something?"

He laughed somewhat nervously and said, "I will do my best. What's on your mind?"

Angeline shifted onto her side facing him. "Have you ever thought about just getting up and leaving for the city?"

"I guess the thought's crossed my mind before, but I've never been very serious about it. I mean, I'm about to take my father's place at the church, so I can't just up and leave. Too many people are depending on me."

She sighed. "Yeah I understand, but I feel like I have to get out of here and see someplace that's different, try new things and have new experiences. Lockwell's suffocating me."

Darl folded the pillow in half and put it under his head then looked her in the eyes. "The idea of moving to the city seems romantic and all, but our friends and family are here in Lockwell. We've already built a life here."

She kissed him and then fell back onto her pillow. "Never mind. I shouldn't have brought it up. Let's talk about something else."

Darl shrugged. "Okay, if you say so."

He awoke covered in sweat, his legs bound in a tangled mess of bedsheets. He'd been dreaming about her again. It'd happened every night since he learned of her death. He was thankful this one was merely a reliving of past events in their relationship, not another hideous nightmare like the night before the funeral. Those visions were too awful to erase from his mind. Images of her mercilessly tormented, burning in hellfire screaming his name, and him powerless to do anything but watch in horror.

So Darl did the only thing he could. He lied, not for selfish gain but out of mercy. He couldn't tell the Blackwoods the truth and destroy what was left of a family that had already lost her twice. First, when she had forsaken her faith and retreated over the state line for the bustling city of Arish. Then a second time, when they learned of her death by heroin overdose in a grimy back alleyway. No, this terrible revelation would remain with him alone, his own private cross to bear.

He sat up in his bed and looked around the room but there was only darkness. A pungent odor filled his nostrils, one that took him a few seconds to recognize as the stench of burnt hair and flesh. He climbed out of bed and sleepily stumbled down the hallway into the kitchen to check the stove but it wasn't on. By now his eyes had adjusted to the faint moonlight spilling through the kitchen window but he saw no smoke.

He reluctantly returned to bed and as he slid back under the covers a macabre thought crossed his mind, causing him to shiver involuntarily. He wouldn't allow himself to fully contemplate it, though, so he forced it back down into his subconscious and closed his eyes, praying for sleep to return.

The next morning Darl gave the conclusion to a series of sermons he'd taught over the last several Sundays about God's redeeming love. He quoted from Psalms 103:

"The Lord is merciful and gracious, slow to anger, and plenteous in mercy. He will not always chide: neither will he keep his anger for ever. He hath not dealt with us after our sins; nor rewarded us according to our iniquities. For as the heaven is high above the earth, so great is his mercy toward them that fear him. As far as the east is from the west, so far hath he removed our transgressions from us."

The message was well-received and afterwards there was a communal lunch for the entire church prepared by several ladies in the congregation. It was a joyful occasion that was much needed in the small church-town that still mourned the loss of one of their own. Darl felt relieved to see smiling faces and hear laughter once again among his flock. He truly loved these people and treated each of them as if they were family. He wandered around the cramped dining hall, playfully teasing the children and shaking hands with members of the choir.

When he returned home that evening it was a different story altogether. The guilt, anxiety, and sadness came back in full force. He was plagued with memories of Angeline and things he should've said and done to make her stay or that might've saved her soul, but now it was much too late. The following evenings only offered more of the same, restless nights spent replaying reels of happier times.

The days weren't much better, either. He turned to the Word for comfort but it only made things worse. Parables of sinners cast into furnaces of fire with the wailing and gnashing of teeth or of a man tormented by the flames begging for a drop of water to cool his tongue. For the type of spiritual anguish he felt, there seemed to be no relief. Even the initial solace of the company of his parish members began to gnaw away at him, especially if it was one of the Blackwoods. Every time he saw one of their cheerful faces growing better by the day he was reminded of the terrible secret he had to endure alone.

"Darl, I honestly don't know how you put up with that man. He's so nosy and judgmental."

"I put up with *that man* because he's my father and he only wants what's best for us." Darl pulled out a chair and took a seat at the kitchen table as Angeline began heating up a pot of water on the stove.

"You mean, he wants what *he* thinks is best for us. You're a grown man – he should let you make your own decisions."

Darl sighed and shook his head. "You just don't get it. I want the same thing that he does. You're the one that wants to move out to Arish, I never said that I did. This place is my home, this *church* is my home. I grew up in those pews and now I want to give back to it and help it prosper in the future."

She threw her head back in a huff and turned to him with a hand defiantly propped on her hip. "God, you really are nothing but his little clone. *'Yes, daddy, whatever you say, daddy.'* Have you ever had an original thought, or do you let your father and that damn book do all the thinking for you?"

He stared back at her with anger in his eyes. "And just what is that supposed to mean?"

"It means you do what everyone else tells you to do. You don't even consider that there could be other possibilities in your life or if it's what you really want. You took the easiest path handed to you. Your father was a pastor, so you became a pastor. You didn't even start your own church, you're just taking over his position because he's retiring.

"And yes," she continued, "there are some nice ideas in the Bible, but it doesn't mean every single thing applies to your life today. We live in a different world now, with automobiles and jazz music. Women are no longer their husbands' property – we actually have the right to vote now. And there are so many different religions out there claiming to be the one and only truth. What makes you so sure this one is right? Because it's the one you were raised with? And how can a book written by a wandering desert tribe a couple thousand years ago tell you how to navigate through life today?"

Darl sat there, completely stunned. "Who are you and what have you done with Angeline?"

She stared back at him for several uncomfortably long seconds, then said, "Darl, I hate to break it to you but I've been this way for quite a while. I kept hoping that you would come around on your own but you become more and more like your father every day. And I've already seen where that road leads and I need something more. I can't stay here and drown in this little backwoods town with you. Not when there's a whole world out there to be had, full of new and exciting experiences."

Darl was crushed. She could see it in his eyes. "You used to love our church and this little backwoods town – what changed all of that?"

She then realized how cruel she sounded. She turned off the stove and sat down beside him at the table, placing her hand over his. "I'm sorry. I didn't want to tell you like this. It sort of just came out. I was waiting for the right time, but it never came."

He exhaled heavily. "When did you start thinking like this?"

Angeline dropped her head and stared at her feet, then looked back up into his eyes. "It's hard to say. I'd had a lot of questions as a kid, but I guess a lot of it came from my Aunt Trudy. She lived in Arish and she used to come visit us and tell us all about the exciting things happening in the big city. So one day I found my father's old Encyclopedia Britannica set and began reading about city life. Then I ended up reading about other world religions – before then I thought everyone was Christian. I didn't even know there were other options."

Darl spoke quietly, his voice barely above a whisper now. "If you didn't believe in God and you always planned to leave Lockwell, why did you even allow me to start courting you?"

Now it was her turn to look hurt. "I never said I didn't believe in God. I'm just not so sure it's the God that's in that book. And I wasn't quite sure what I thought about anything when we first started courting, Darl. The only thing I was sure about was that I cared for you."

"… and now you don't." He was no longer looking into her eyes but gazing out the kitchen window at something she couldn't see.

A single tear fell from her eye leaving a trail down her cheek. "That's not true."

Darl finally returned to meet her eyes again. "So then where does that leave us?"

"I … I don't know, Darl. I just don't know … "

He found himself lying in bed once again, the room filled with an impenetrable darkness. The acrid smell of burnt flesh and hair from the other night had returned. Now it was much stronger than before, almost stinging his nostrils with its potency. His eyes roamed back and forth desperately, attempting to adjust in the low light. Soon a dim rectangle began to take shape. It was the doorway that lead down the hall to his kitchen.

Initially, he was relieved to make out anything at all until he saw the silhouette of a figure standing in the hallway. He found himself unable to move, completely paralyzed with fear. His breathing came out in short, shallow bursts as his heart began to pound uncontrollably. He waited for the form to proceed down the hallway toward him but it stood motionless. After several minutes passed with no change he had gathered the courage to speak.

"H-Hello? Is anyone there?" The panic in his voice was more than apparent but it was the best he could do.

Darl waited for a response and a long, raspy sigh rose up from the hall. The figure drifted closer, appearing to glide over the floor rather than requiring the movement of its lower extremities. The hair on his arms and legs stood erect as he shrunk back in horror. It was now crossing the threshold into the room with him. Where eyes should've been there were glowing, orange embers and the hair hung in uneven, ragged clumps from its head. As it neared his bedside he recognized the blackened, fissured face all too well. It was Angeline.

He closed his eyes, hoping that when he reopened them the apparition would be gone. Instead it had drawn even closer with its hand outstretched for him, only inches from his face. Her mouth opened wide as if to speak and thick plumes of smoke poured forth. Her body began to convulse as it burst into flames.

With this, something inside him finally broke. His eyes flooded with tears as he collapsed back onto the bed, screaming up at the ceiling. "How could You let this happen to her? You claimed to love her even more than I did. You liar! I wouldn't wish this on my worst enemy and You did this to one of Your children? She didn't know. She was just confused like all of us, but there are no excuses good enough, are there? It's simply turn or burn! You say, *'Depart from me, I never knew you.'* Well, now I truly know You … and I wish we'd never met."

He closed his eyes tight whispering, "I'm sorry, I'm so sorry. I should've done more, I always thought there would be more time. That eventually you'd come back around, but now it's too late. You were my responsibility and I failed you. Now I see, this is my punishment … I would trade places with you if only I could."

He lay there completely still, waiting for the awful touch of those charred, dead hands but it never came. When he opened his eyes again the room was empty and quiet. Darkness had resumed, only now it was different, somehow comforting.

He didn't know why but he had been spared …

****

Several weeks had passed since Darl's last vision of Angeline and much had changed in his life. He'd resigned from his position at the church. Saying goodbye to his congregation was one of the hardest things he'd ever done. It was as if he was leaving his second family without the courtesy of even telling them why, but he knew some of them had guessed at the truth. He'd left it up to his father to find another replacement.

At home he'd spent the last two days packing his things in boxes and loading them into the back of the pickup truck Josiah had loaned him for the move. He'd gotten a lease on a small, one-bedroom apartment in the city and decided to try his hand as a file clerk at the local library. It was a quiet, unassuming job with a measly paycheck, but at least it was something. It was a strange feeling, arranging his life into small cardboard boxes and uprooting himself to an unfamiliar place, but he knew it had to be done.

Aside from the occasional lapses into nostalgia, he discovered he was quite adept at the whole moving process. One of his more solemn reflections came when he had to pack up his mother's ring that was meant for the woman he'd marry. He allowed the emotions to flow through him and pass unashamed. As he put the last box in the bed of the small pickup he saw Josiah walking up the dirt path to him.

"Hey Darl, need a hand?"

Darl smiled and put his hand on the box closest to him. "Actually, that was the last one, but thanks."

Josiah laughed. "Leave it up to old Josiah to offer his help right when you finish, huh?"

"Nah, you've already done plenty. If you'd like you can give me a ride back to the apartment so you can get your truck back tonight."

"All right. Sounds like a plan," Josiah said as he opened the door and climbed into the driver's seat of the small pickup truck.

"Give me a few minutes to do one last check and make sure I didn't miss anything."

Josiah nodded his consent and Darl went back into the house. He glanced in each room but saw nothing until he reached the den. There on the floor he spotted the worn cover of his old bible blanketed in a thin layer of dust. He took a step toward it then hesitated as a memory flooded his mind.

It was early on in the relationship, he and Angeline had stayed up talking about their ambitions and future plans late into the night and she'd fallen asleep in his grandmother's rocking chair. He'd carried her to his bed and tucked her in planning to make a place for himself on the sofa. Before he turned out the light he turned to catch one last glimpse of her and he found himself captivated by her serene beauty. Her face told of a tranquil sleep as if she had never known hardship and could only dream of pleasant things.

This face with its smooth features and quiet composure was how he always wanted to remember her. He turned around and calmly exited the den. He already had everything he needed from this place.

Darl climbed into the passenger side of the truck and Josiah turned to him and said, "Ready?"

He smiled and shook his head. "I'm ready."

Josiah stepped on the pedal and moved the throttle lever into gear and they were off.

LE RENARD NOIR

I sneak quietly, quietly through the woods
Swim across the creek and through the meadow
The moonlight as my only guide

I smell him, I know he's here
I hear him rustling underground
I'll follow him to an entrance
And lie in wait to ambush him there

I find it
Facedown in the tall grass
Breathing slowly, wind whispers through the weeds
I start to drift, but something brings me back
His head pokes through
And I'm up in the air before I even realize it

A short struggle and it's over in moments
I think of her, back home, tending to the children
And how proud she'll be of me
I drag him back toward the woods, retracing my steps

I reach the black, stretching path of the beast
Like the one that took my brother long ago
This is always the worst part
I begin to cross then I see its glowing eyes
Coming up over the hill and descending quickly upon me

I can hear it growling, always an angry, steady roar
For a second I freeze, caught in its glare
Its eyes locked with mine
Then I dart forward and leap from the path
It screams by in frustration, barely missing me
And continues on its way

I sigh with relief
And head back through the woods
Towards my love with my prize
She'll be so proud of me ...

THE DOORWAY
IN THE GARDEN

Osyka sat on the back porch reading a Star Wars book as her grandmother, Melinda, tended the garden.

"Pokni?"

Melinda lifted her head, wiping the sweat from her brow with the back of her gloved hand. "Yes, dear?"

"Do you think Dad is in Heaven?"

Melinda sighed. "Yes, sweetheart. I believe your father is with Jesus now."

Osyka frowned. "But Dad said Jesus is the white people's god, not ours."

"Jesus is everyone's God, dear."

"Well, that's not what Dad said."

Melinda put her hand rake down. "Osyka, your father was smart, but he didn't know everything. Tom grew up—"

Osyka gave her grandmother a look of disapproval.

Melinda shook her head. "Sorry. *Nashoba* grew up in a time when people were first becoming proud to call themselves Indian, which is a wonderful thing, don't get me wrong. You should never be ashamed of your family's heritage, but I think some people take it a little too far, like your parents. I'm a Christian first, then I'm a Choctaw. Not everything the white man has taught us has been evil; Indians do evil quite well when left to their own. You would do well to remember that."

Osyka heard the phone ring from the open sliding glass door that led into the kitchen. Her grandmother stood up and said, "I better go get that, dear. Don't get into any trouble." She walked up the wooden stairs of the porch and continued into the house.

Osyka sat her book down on the porch swing and stepped down into her grandmother's elaborate garden. The garden behind her house was Melinda's pride and joy. It had become her main focus after the death of her husband, Albert, two decades before. Albert had been a Choctaw Code Talker in the Second World War and was fifteen years her senior. They'd had a long, loving marriage and his death sent her into a deep depression that even her church family was unable to pull her out of. Then her daughter-in-law, Biskane, mentioned that she'd read somewhere that keeping a garden was a good way to combat depression and helped to promote inner peace.

Melinda had initially scoffed and wrote it off as another one of her son and daughter-in-law's silly, New Age remedies, but when she finally gave it a chance she discovered a newfound passion in her life. Within a year the garden was flourishing and she held a closer relationship with Biskane than ever before. Osyka loved exploring her grandmother's garden whenever they visited. It had been around longer than she'd been alive and she enjoyed seeing each new addition made to it.

The garden covered the entire expanse of the backyard leading up to the wooded area beyond it. Her grandmother had placed an assortment of antique curiosities around the garden to give it a whimsical air. Decorative lanterns and hummingbird feeders hung from the gnarled branches of sturdy trees. There was a footpath made of small stepping stones lined with potted plants and shrubs sprouting from the ground. Off to each side were small brightly-colored benches utilizing the best vantage points within. Osyka's favorite part of all, though, was the little wooden bridge over the tiny stream with a beautiful wrought iron arch demarcating the end of the garden from the woods.

To Osyka's fanciful young mind, the arch was the doorway to a fantasy world. A world where adventures awaited and all things were possible, yet Melinda forbid her of ever crossing it, reminding her of the dangers of the woods and the wildlife inhabiting it. Her grandmother was unaware that Osyka had already accompanied her father and brother on several hunting trips and if she had known, she would have strongly disapproved. Even so, the woods behind her Pokni's house seemed different than the other woods she'd been in. They were enchanted somehow, possibly due to their forbidden status. She stared out at them, mesmerized by the hum of the cicadas, as she imagined all of the forest creatures roaming within.

She could faintly hear bits of the conversation her grandmother was having on the phone inside. "… did they let you see him? How's he doing? … That poor boy, no one should ever have to endure that … He was up there all alone for weeks … That's awful … "

Osyka knew they were talking about her older brother, Koi. She hadn't seen him for nearly two months since he and her father had flown out to get Biskane's mother, Namid, Osyka's grandmother on the opposite side of the family. Biskane was an Ojibwe from Canada who'd lived in the United States since her early twenties, but when she learned of Namid's failing health, Nashoba and Koi agreed to fly up and bring her down to Mississippi to live with the rest of the family.

Then there was the Crash.

"Osyka, it's getting dark. Time to come inside."

After dinner Osyka sat at the table watching the storm clouds through the sliding glass doors as Melinda washed the dishes. The rain came suddenly, cascading onto the roof and windows with such force that Osyka feared the glass would break. Melinda paused between dishes to stare out the window above the sink. "Wow, I haven't seen a downpour like that in years."

As if in response to her words, the lights flickered then went out. Melinda stood at the sink with a plate and a towel in her hand, unable to see anything as her eyes struggled to adjust. There was a brilliant flash of light, in which she caught a glimpse of Osyka's panicked face, followed by a deep rumbling that shook the entire house.

Through the darkness she heard Osyka's voice. "I'm scared, Pokni."

"There's no reason to be scared, dear. I've got some candles. I'll set one at the table and tell you a story about where the thunder and lightning come from. How does that sound?"

"Sounds good."

The candles cast shadows upon their faces as Melinda recounted the tale of Heloha and Melatha, the two giant birds responsible for the violent thunderstorms above. Osyka giggled as she imagined Heloha's enormous eggs rumbling across the cloud tops and Melatha streaking through the sky desperately attempting to catch them before they fell to the Earth. She felt better after her grandmother's story and agreed to let Melinda tuck her into bed for the night.

Melinda kissed her on the forehead, wishing her a

goodnight's rest. Osyka smiled in response before falling fast asleep.

She awoke to the sound of someone crying. She had no idea how late it was, but she knew a significant amount of time had passed since the candle her grandmother had left was almost entirely burned away. She glanced at the clock on her bedside table but the electronic display was blank. The power was still out. Her throat was parched so she decided to get a glass of water. The crying grew louder as she passed her grandmother's bedroom on the way to the kitchen.

Osyka pressed her ear against the door and heard her grandmother whispering between sobs, "Why? Why must my family endure this? I'll always trust You, but I just don't understand. I know Albert lived a full life, but why did You have to take my son so soon? He had a wife and kids, still so much to live for. I just don't understand, Lord."

She'd heard her grandmother speak with God before, but never like this. She sounded angry and hurt. Osyka wanted to go in and hug her but she was afraid she'd be upset about her being up so late. She decided to continue on to the kitchen. She stood on her tiptoes and pulled a coffee mug from the cabinet above the stovetop and filled it with water from the sink faucet. Through the sliding glass doors she stared out at her grandmother's garden illuminated by moonlight.

Then she saw it.

Something stood up from the bench in the garden and walked in the direction of the woods. She pressed her face against the glass to get a better look, cupping her hands above her eyes to avoid any glares. There was no doubt about it. It was her brother, Koi. She could plainly see his long, dark hair, the serpent tattoo coiling around his forearm, and his sleeveless denim jacket covered in band patches.

What's he doing out there? He didn't even let me and Pokni know he was back, she thought.

He turned and looked back at her before heading across the bridge, through the arch, and into the woods. Osyka slid the door open and descended the back porch into the garden. As she hurried over the stepping stones to the bridge, she spoke in a hushed yet frantic tone, "Koi! Koi, stop! Come back here."

She hesitated when she made it to the wooden bridge, considering all of her grandmother's warnings throughout her life. *But I've got to know why Koi's here,* she thought. *He seemed like he wanted me to follow him.*

Osyka made her decision.

There was the crunch of dry leaves under her feet as she passed through the arch, leaving her grandmother's garden behind for the first time. Nothing seemed particularly unusual or exciting about the woods; there was only an eerie silence. She continued on, pushing several low hanging branches out of her face.

"Koi, where are you? Wait for me."

There was no response.

Something rustled through the undergrowth nearby. "Hello? Koi, is that you?"

A piercing cry rang out in the night, causing her to shudder as if an icepick had run a course down her spine, jabbing each individual vertebra along the way. At first she thought it was a woman screaming, but she quickly realized she'd heard this sound before.

A year earlier she'd been sitting on the back porch with her father when a similar cry had echoed through the woods. Osyka was frightened but Nashoba calmed her, informing her it was merely the call of a fox searching for a mate. A response from another fox soon followed and her father smiled and said, "Sounds like he found one."

The pleasant memory put her at ease but as the minutes passed and the silence resumed, Osyka recalled the legend of the shilombish. Every person has a *shilup*, or soul, that goes on to the land of ghosts after death, but each person also has a *shilombish*, or shadow, as well. If the dead person had unfinished business or was troubled, the shilombish would remain on the earth haunting the areas it was familiar with in life. The shilombish would often assume the form of an owl or a fox, and its cry was considered a bad omen for anyone who heard it. One could distinguish the cry of the shilombish from an actual fox or owl by its lack of a response, as foxes and owls often cry to one another in the night.

Osyka grew apprehensive as she scoured the darkness for anything unusual. Then she saw the pair of glowing eyes staring back at her through the gloom. As she looked on, a thick formation of clouds rolled away and the moonlight revealed a black fox sitting beneath a tree, with its large tail flicking ever so lightly back and forth across its body.

She decided to extend it a peace offering. "Mr. Shilombish, please let me pass. I don't want any trouble. I'm just trying to find my brother, Koi. I saw him wander in here and as soon as I get him, we'll leave you and your woods alone. I promise."

Aside from its waving tail the fox remained still, as if considering her offer. Then it silently rose on all fours and scampered off in the opposite direction.

"Thank you," Osyka called after it.

She continued searching the area and calling out to her

brother but he was nowhere to be found. After a while she decided to turn back but she was no longer sure of which way she'd come from. No matter the direction she faced, there was only an endless expanse of trees. Though she was now officially lost in the woods at night she felt unusually calm about the situation. So she sat down in front of a large tree and laid back resting her head against its trunk.

When she awoke it was daylight and she was in her pajamas from the night before. A thick blanket of branches, leaves, and other vegetation covered her, keeping her warm. Immediately she thought of Koi and sat up to search her surroundings but found no one.

A rock collided with the tree trunk, narrowly missing her head. "What the … ? Hey, who's out there!?"

She heard someone snickering, followed by a rustling in the bushes ahead.

"Oh, you think that's funny, do you? Well, let's see how funny it is when it happens to you." Osyka picked up the rock and chucked it hard back into the bushes. There was a loud thump and the movement ceased as a little man fell out of the foliage.

She pushed the blanket of branches aside and cautiously approached the little man to get a better look at him. He was about two feet tall with long, gray hair and skin that was tanned dark and rough as leather. He was dressed in a hodgepodge of furs of various forest animals and lay so still that she feared she might've killed him.

"Oh, please don't be dead. I didn't mean to hurt you, little man. I was just angry because you laughed at me. Plus, you did throw that rock first."

She was on the verge of crying when she noticed the

steady rise and fall of his chest. Without warning, he jumped to his feet with his fists up in a defensive gesture. Osyka screamed and the little man leapt onto her back and put a hand over her mouth. She was about to fling him off when she saw his other hand motioning to a large black bear only twenty feet away.

The bear looked at them curiously and took a few steps in their direction with its snout held high, sniffing the air. It clawed the ground, snorted loudly, and lowered its head. Osyka's mind raced through several scenarios, trying to determine a good course of action. Before she could make a decision the little man hopped down and ran at the bear screaming and waving his hands around. The bear looked at him somewhat amused at first, then quickly grew annoyed as the man began throwing rocks at it. For a few seconds it appeared the black bear was going to stand its ground and fight, but then decided it wasn't worth the effort and retreated to another part of the woods.

When the little man returned Osyka said, "I know who you are. You're one of the *kowi anukasha*."

He looked at her and shrugged his shoulders.

The little man turned and started to walk away when Osyka called after him. "Hey, have you seen my brother? His name is Koi. I followed him into these woods last night but then he disappeared. He's tall and skinny with long black hair, and he always wears a raggedy jacket."

The little man stopped and looked at her then nodded his head and waved for her to follow him.

"Oh, you have seen him? That's great! Which way was he heading?"

The little man continued walking, giving her no response.

Oh, well, she thought, *hopefully he'll just take me to Koi if he knows where he is.*

As time dragged on, Osyka started to wonder where he was actually leading her. "Hey, you are taking me to my brother, right?" As she finished the question they reached the top of a hill and the little man pointed to the entrance of a cave at the bottom of the slope in the forest floor.

"Koi's in there?" she asked, a bit skeptical.

The little man pointed again, emphatically this time, impatient with her persistent questioning.

"All right, all right. No need to get upset."

She made her way down the slope, careful not to slip on the dead leaves covering the hillside. She paused when she reached the cave entrance to look back at the little man, but he was gone. She turned and stared into the mouth of the cave, reconsidering her decision as she gazed into the darkness. A flame burst to life from within and Osyka nearly fell with surprise until she saw it was only the little man with a large torch.

"Wait!? How did you … ?"

She realized it didn't matter as he welcomed her inside. As they walked further into the cavern she saw that the walls were covered in simple yet beautiful paintings of forest creatures, some that were familiar to her and many that weren't. There were also several handcrafted clay cups and dishes, as well as a makeshift bed constructed out of tree limbs and animal skins.

"This is your home, isn't it?"

He smiled, nodding his head yes, as they ventured on. They came to a pool of water that was an offshoot of a larger subterranean lake when he turned and handed the torch to her and took several steps back. Osyka listened to the torch flicker and pop as she examined the calm, clear water. There was a ripple as something moved beneath the surface and a figure rose from the pool. It had long, white hair and a pale shroud draped over its emaciated body. It slowly approached her with a dagger clasped in its hands.

Osyka was about to turn and run when she realized the figure was not trying to attack her but was rather offering the dagger to her. It stopped a few feet before her, holding the dagger with its handle facing her. She was tempted to reach out and take it but something told her to wait, a vague recollection of a story about the kowi anukasha she was told as a toddler. The little forest-dwelling people were known for giving children trials of great significance to their paths in life. She needed to wait; there would be more.

As she finished the thought another figure, identical to the first, rose out of the water with its hands outstretched. This one offered a coil of black, twisted roots and herbs in its palms. *Keep waiting,* she thought.

The third figure emerged about a minute later, with hands full of lively roots and fragrant green herbs. *Here it is.* She reached out and gently plucked them from its hands. The three figures smiled pleasantly, sighing in unison. The first two tucked the contents of their hands into the folds of their shrouds as the third spoke in a surprisingly gentle voice.

"You are wise beyond your years, my child. If you had accepted the dagger, you would've been destined to become a slaughterer of your people. If you had taken the black herbs you would've been an unsuccessful doctor but, alas, you made the wise decision and waited for the third gift. So we three spirits will teach you the secrets of making natural medicines to cure the sicknesses and ailments of your people. You will become a great doctor with time."

The little man stepped forward and patted her on the back. Over the course of the next few days she learned from the spirits and the little man the types of herbs, roots, and barks to save the Choctaw from all manners of diseases. Osyka was shown how to make an herbal tea to cure stomach aches. She was instructed how to make natural salves and healing balms for cuts and scrapes. She also learned how to properly clean and dress wounds. As her training drew to a close, she thanked them all but said she must continue on and find her brother. They wished her well and gave her a bag made of buckskin filled with materials to make natural medicines.

As Osyka left the cave behind she worried that she had spent too much time with the kowi anukasha and the three spirits. Koi might be long gone now, so far away that she'd never be able to catch up with him, but something told her to press on in spite of her doubts. She walked in the direction she'd last seen him going. After several hours of trudging through tall grass, over fallen trees, and up steep hills she came upon a great river.

I wonder if this is the Mississippi, she thought as she stared into the river's dark, churning water as it passed. On the opposing bank she saw an old canoe with a paddle sticking up out of it. *That's got to be Koi's. Well, at least I know I'm heading the right way now.*

She was going to have to swim to the other side if she wanted to stay on his trail. Osyka made sure her buckskin bag was fastened tight as she waded out into the muddied waters. She steeled her nerves then began to breaststroke toward the opposite shore. In the middle of the river the current was at its strongest and it took all the energy she had to keep from being swept downstream. As exhaustion was about to overcome her she reached a spot that was calm and cool.

She barely had to kick her legs to maintain her position in the river, and though this was a welcome relief for her tired extremities, it made little sense as she watched the current flowing violently around her. She began to shiver as she realized that not only was the water colder in this particular area but it was also unusually clear. She was able to see all the way down to the bottom of the riverbed.

Something hard brushed against her leg.

She saw a flash of speckled white skin and assumed it was a fish until a webbed hand wrapped around her ankle. She kicked at it, trying to free herself, but soon she was dragged beneath the surface. She looked below to identify her assailant and saw a pair of glassy, bulging eyes staring back at her out of a humanoid face covered in scales. The *okwa naholo*, or white people of the water, had her now. If she didn't escape its grasp soon it would drag her all the way down to its home and she would have to live as one of them.

No, I've got to help my brother! This isn't the way things are supposed to go.

As she struggled in its grasp she noticed the creature wore a belt with a sheathed hunting dagger around its waist. As it dragged her deeper she was afraid her lungs might burst until she realized that as long as it held her she could breathe in the water. This meant the transformation was already occurring; there wasn't much time left. She reached down and placed her hand over its wrist, causing it to pause and look up at her. She thrust her thumb into the creature's eye and it coiled in pain, bringing the hunting dagger around its waist within her reach.

Osyka grabbed the knife by the handle, pulled it free from

its sheath, and raised it high above her head. As she brought the knife down, as if to stab it, the creature released her. She kicked her arms and legs frantically as she shot back up to the top. Her head broke through the surface of the water and she gasped for air as she swam to shore. She collapsed facedown at the riverbank with the hunting dagger in her hand and the buckskin bag around her neck.

She was glad she hadn't had to seriously hurt the okwa naholo. The mere threat of violence had been enough for it to let go of her. She looked back and saw its head peeking up from the water, watching her. She waved in a mock-friendly manner then stretched out on the shore. The sun was setting now, hues of pink and orange crawled across the evening sky.

Osyka's stomach rumbled as she noticed a slight chill in the air. It was going to get cold soon and she needed food and warmth. She looked down at the hunting knife still in her hand. *All right, I guess it's time to put this to some use,* she thought.

Though it was against her mother's wishes, Nashoba sometimes allowed Osyka to accompany them on the hunting trips he and Koi had each year. Biskane believed that shooting guns and the killing and cleaning of deer were not proper activities for a young woman to learn, but her father felt that deer hunting was an important tradition of their people that he should pass along to both of his children. Osyka was grateful for the knowledge and experience now that she had no other options, but she'd never killed a deer with only a hunting knife; this wasn't going to be easy.

She started off scouring the woods for "scrapes," telltale spots where bucks had cleared the forest floor and urinated as a means to attract does that were ready to mate. Mature bucks used scrapes as a calling card to alert does to their presence in an area as well as a way to intimidate subordinate bucks that might consider competing with them. Osyka found a seemingly well-trafficked scrape before determining it was in a poor location for her to hide and wait. She'd need to move it to a place where she would be downwind of approaching deer with a better vantage point.

Nashoba had taught her and Koi how to make mock scrapes when necessary. First, she needed to take the "licking branch" from a scrape. The licking branch was an essential part, some would argue the most essential part, of any successful scrape. Bucks rubbed their facial scent glands on the branch and the does licked it to learn about the buck that made it. Osyka liked to think of scrapes as deer community bulletin boards. They used them as a way to keep track of each other when they shared an area of the forest.

She broke off the worn licking branch and carried it over to a location she could use to an advantage. She tied the licking branch to the trunk of a tree using dead roots she'd found. Then she cleared a spot of ground beneath it of dead leaves and branches. Finally, in order to stir up the curiosity of any passing deer, she peed on the ground. Some hunters believed this was foolish because you were deliberately alerting the deer to your presence, but her father swore by it. So, of course, she did as well.

She climbed up high into the tree and prepared for what would most likely be a very long wait. She was amazed when in less than an hour she saw a young doe cautiously approaching her mock scrape below. Osyka readied herself, knowing she'd have to act in the exact right moment to drop down on the deer from above and perform a swift clean cut across its throat in order to kill the animal as quickly and mercifully as possible. The doe was stepping into position when a high-pitched scream rang out, spooking the deer and nearly causing Osyka to fall out of the tree.

As the doe darted away Osyka looked around for the source of the scream. At the foot of the tree stood the *kashehotapalo*, a half-man, half-deer creature, smiling fiendishly back up at her. This spirit was known to taunt and frustrate hunters, but this was her first time encountering it. It scampered off laughing through the trees, and as her stomach grumbled with hunger she vowed revenge.

Osyka knew it was unlikely she'd see another deer tonight, especially after the kashehotapalo had scared off every nearby animal, but she decided to stay up in the tree anyway. She got as comfortable as she could and nestled herself between two branches at chest level that would help prop her up and keep her from falling out of the tree. As she waited, she watched the red-orange moon peek over the eastern horizon, and she remembered thinking it was beautiful … .

A branch breaking below startled her; the moon was now high in the western sky. As her eyes grew more accustomed to the darkness she saw the antlers of a large buck sniffing around her scrape. She silently positioned herself above and slightly ahead of the animal as she withdrew the hunting knife. Before she dropped down she saw the black fox dart out in front of the swiftly approaching kashehotapalo, tripping it. The buck lifted its head at the commotion as she dragged the hunting knife down through its neck. The panicked animal bolted several yards away then collapsed face-first into a ditch.

Osyka sprinted after it and placed her hand on its side, whispering, "It's okay now, it's okay." As its legs slowly stopped kicking, she thanked the buck for the gift of its life and allowing her to go on. She saw the kashehotapalo rise to its feet, glaring angrily back at her as it slunk away in defeat. She also saw the glowing eyes and flicking tail of the shilombish as it placidly observed her with the fresh kill.

Had it intentionally helped her? And if so, why?

Maybe it wants to share the kill, she reasoned. She waved her hand, motioning for it to come over. "Come on, we can share it."

The fox remained where it was, quietly watching her from afar.

"Okay, suit yourself. Thanks for the help, Mr. Shilombish."

She quickly got to work cleaning and skinning the deer. Afterwards, she made a fire to cook the meat and smoke-tanned the hide so she could use it for warmth as she traveled further north. It was nearing sunrise when Osyka finally sat to take the first bites of the deer meat she'd cooked. As she brought it to her lips the black fox leapt up at her, then paced back and forth whining impatiently. She held some meat out to it. "Here, I told you we could share."

The fox wouldn't accept it, though; it just kept whining and motioned in a particular direction with its head.

"Are you wanting me to follow you?"

It barked in response to her.

"Okay, let me finish eating and I'll see whatever you want to show me."

It barked again.

"Seriously? This can't wait?"

It whined and motioned with its head again.

"All right. This better be good because I'm *really* hungry."

She stuffed some of the cooked deer meat in her bag, just in case, but she fully intended on coming back for the rest of the meat and the hide, especially after all the work she'd put into it. She hurried behind the black fox as it led her to a shallow stream. A melancholy song carried across the water as it trickled over the rocks. A morning mist hovered above everything and the sun began to break through the treetops. Osyka looked upstream through the morning fog and saw a woman dressed in white with flowers in her hair stepping from the water. She followed the woman back into the trees and watched as she stepped upon a large mound of earth, all the while singing the same sad, haunting song.

Osyka approached her. "Why do you sound so sad?"

Without a hint of surprise, the woman in white calmly turned to her and replied, "I'm very hungry. I can't remember the last time I had something to eat."

Join the club, Osyka thought as her stomach grumbled loudly.

"Do you have anything I could eat?" the woman said with pleading eyes.

Osyka reached into the bag and held the deer meat out to her. "Here take this, I've got plenty more back there."

The woman devoured the venison without even stopping to take breaths. When she was finished she held Osyka by the hands and said, "Thank you, I don't know what I would've done without you. I might've starved to death."

Osyka smiled sheepishly back at her. "Oh, it was nothing."

The woman stared deep into her eyes. "Your generosity will not be forgotten. Return to this spot tomorrow evening and you will be rewarded."

The cry of the shilombish echoed through the woods once again. Osyka turned to look and when she turned back the woman in white had vanished. She stood on the mound of earth alone. She decided it was time to return to her fire and the deer she'd prepared. When she made it back she saw a pack of wolves finishing off the last scraps of the deer carcass.

"No, no, NOOOOO!"

She chased after them as they scattered in every direction. She fell to her knees and cried. *It's all that stupid shilombish's fault,* she thought. Why had he helped her catch the deer, only to then distract her from eating it? He must've wanted her to help the woman in white and she was happy to do it but she might be the one that starved now. She stared up at the early morning sun but didn't feel much warmth. It was growing colder and it appeared that Koi's trail was leading her even further north. She was going to need more layers.

The deer hide was still hanging where she'd left it; at least the wolves hadn't run off with that as well. She pulled the hide down and wrapped herself in it. She hadn't slept much last night so she was getting drowsy from exhaustion. She curled up in front of the glowing embers of her fire and stuffed her bag beneath her head using the hide as a blanket. It didn't take long for sleep to come.

It was late in the day when Osyka awoke this time. She got up and gathered her things before pouring water on the embers to make sure they were truly dead and unable to ignite anything on the nearby forest floor. She stuck around for a little while to be sure then started off on her journey anew.

She hadn't made it very far when the woman in white's words came back to her, "Return to this spot tomorrow evening and you will be rewarded."

It's probably nothing, she thought, *but it wouldn't hurt to check.*

It took a few minutes to locate the mound but when she did she was surprised to see a fully grown cornstalk with several ears of corn hanging from it. *How in the world did that pop up over night?* It was a strange occurrence, but surely not the strangest thing she'd seen on this trip, by far. She decided to not question it too much and accept the change in her fortune.

She removed an ear of corn and shucked it before devouring the entire cob. The corn was sweet and crisp, causing her to reach for another ear with a renewed hunger. As she pulled the second ear from the stalk she noticed another one had grown where she'd removed the first cob from.

"No way!"

As she bit into the second corn cob she watched another one sprout from the stalk and rapidly grow in the empty space it had left. She proceeded to fill her bag with corn, watching it sprout as quickly as she could pluck it from the stalk. Now she realized who the woman in white was. It was Ohoyo Osh Chisba, the goddess who brought corn to the Choctaw people. She understood why the shilombish had distracted her and brought her to this place. She didn't know why, but it had been looking out for her once again. The deer she killed would have fed her for only a few meals, but this magical self-renewing corn could feed her indefinitely. She only needed to plant a few kernels and soon she'd have an entire stalk with an endless supply of ears.

Before continuing the search for her brother, she silently thanked the goddess and the mysterious shilombish. Osyka pulled the deer hide up around her shoulders. She'd kept the skull plate where the antlers grew from attached to the hide and placed it on her head, allowing her to wear the hide like a poncho. The antlers served as an intimidating ornament for any animals that might consider attacking her and doubled as a camouflage helping her to blend in with other wildlife. In fact, her camouflage was so successful that she was able to sneak up on the unsuspecting kashehotapalo and frighten it, finally giving it a taste of its own medicine.

As she pressed further north the trees grew increasingly bare and snow and ice covered the ground. She was now entering Ojibwe territory, the land of her mother's people. She didn't know why Koi was taking her this far but she knew she was starting to gain on him, signs of his presence were becoming ever more prominent. There were tracks in the snow leading up the mountainside that she knew were Koi's. What she couldn't figure out though was why the impressions were of his bare feet. Why was he walking through the snow with no shoes?

She followed the tracks into a forest of spruce trees ascending the mountain. A thick mist rose from the trees and she thought of the story of Gawaunduk, an Ojibwe woman who never loved her elderly husband until it was too late. The mist that hovered over forests of spruce were said to be her tears still mourning the husband she had taken for granted in life. Osyka was not as familiar with her Ojibwe heritage as she was with her Choctaw side, thanks to her father's daily teachings, but her mother had passed a few stories down to her children.

The snow grew deeper as she trudged through the trees further up the mountain, so she pulled the deer hide tighter around to conserve her body heat as the temperature dropped with the increase in elevation. In the distance she could hear a faint drumming that seemed to be getting closer. When the drumming reached a crescendo a large gray rabbit hopped out across the snow before her and stopped. She figured if she kept walking the rabbit would get spooked and flee, but instead it sat with its eyes locked onto her own.

Osyka then realized who she was encountering, this was no ordinary rabbit. This was the *manitou*, or Ojibwe spirit, Cheeby-aub-oozoo – the bringer of music and Chief of the Underworld. The drumming was so loud now that she felt as if it was pounding on the inside of her skull. She stared back into the face of Cheeby-aub-oozoo and began to plead the case for her life.

"I'm sorry if I have offended you by entering your sacred domain, Cheeby-aub-oozoo. I mean no harm, I'm only ten years old. I've come here searching for my brother Koi and as soon as I find him we will leave you in peace. Please have mercy on us and let us remain in the land of the living."

There were several tense seconds as she awaited a response. Suddenly, the drumming ceased and the rabbit broke its long held gaze before scampering into the underbrush. Osyka breathed a sigh of relief. She hoped her brother appreciated how many times she'd risked her life for him.

Probably not, she thought with a smile. *Brothers rarely do.*

The wind started to pick up. She needed to keep moving while she still had the energy. There was a full moon in the sky casting the massive shadows of the trees across her path. After Cheeby-aub-oozoo left, the mountain was strangely quiet. For a long period of time all she heard was the *crinch-crunching* of her shoes in the snow and the howl of the wind. Osyka came upon a rocky crag that she would have to scale if she wanted to go any further. She looked for a way around it but there didn't appear to be one.

So she made sure her buckskin bag was fastened securely and started to climb. She focused on placing one hand after the other, one foot after the next and tried not to think about how high she'd gotten or how one simple mistake could send her plummeting to her death. The technique worked and before she knew it she had reached the top. Thick overhanging trees and deep snow resumed along with the raging winds whistling through the branches and yet still no animal sounds.

Maybe they're all smarter than me and hiding from the cold, she thought.

Ahead she saw something splayed out in the snow, as she grew closer she recognized what it was and her heart sank. It was Koi's favorite jacket. *He'd never leave that behind – it's his most prized possession.* It made even less sense that he would get rid of it in this bitter cold. Something must've gone wrong, something bad had happened to him. She picked up the jacket and held it close. She caught a whiff of cheap cigarettes and stale beer; it still smelled like him so it hadn't been here very long.

To her left she heard branches cracking and breaking. The tree trunks creaked as if straining from an immense weight pressing down on top of them, but she saw nothing. The sound of wood twisting and popping grew closer as the wind picked up, the snow fell in sheets. In the corner of her eye she saw something very thin and tall move toward her, but she turned her head and there were only branches swaying.

The snowfall was now reaching blizzard proportions, she was going to need to find cover fast if this kept up for much longer.

Then she saw it.

The Wendigo's obscenely emaciated limbs and brown, weathered skin resembled branches in profile, but as it turned to face her she saw the cracked, receding lips reveal a wicked skull-like grin. The icy, blue eyes were barely visible buried deep within their sockets as it opened its mouth and shrieked, sending a blast of piercing-cold air into her face and hair. Osyka screamed in horror then fled in the opposite direction.

She ran as fast as she could but the snow was getting deeper, making escape all the more difficult. Plus, the thick blanket of snow hid rocks and branches along the way causing her to stumble several times. She didn't have time to turn and check but she knew it was chasing her. Osyka could hear its dry, hollow joints being put to use as it tried to keep up with her.

She saw a bowling ball-sized rock jutting up out of the snow to her left and a large frozen pond beyond that on her right. She quickly formed a plan that might buy her a few minutes. As she came upon the large rock she dug her heels in and dropped to the ground as if she was sliding into home base. The creature was unable to correct its course in time and ran past her, attempted to stop, and collided head-first into a thicket of trees and dead bushes.

Osyka lifted the large rock with both of her hands and heaved it to her chest as the monstrosity regained its footing. She took off once again, this time headed toward the frozen pond. As she approached it she prayed the ice would be thick enough to support her but not thick enough to foil her plan. Her feet hit the icy surface and she nearly lost it but was able to regain some traction. She'd made it halfway across the pond when she heard its feet scraping over the ice behind her.

It's now or never, Osyka.

She let go of the heavy rock and heard the ice crack beneath her as she leapt toward the pond's outer edge. She hit the snowy bank and clambered up the incline as she heard the ice give way. She turned and saw it go under with its impossibly long arms flailing about as it vanished beneath the surface. Osyka knew she hadn't seen the last of the Wendigo, though; it was the most feared creature among the Ojibwe, known for its bloodlust and insatiable hunger. When it discovered prey, it rarely gave up until it had obtained it.

The Wendigo had, at one time, been an ordinary human that was driven to do the unthinkable. Ojibwe territory was known for its harsh terrain and brutal winters when food became so scarce that anyone who hadn't prepared for the long haul was doomed with starvation. Year after year it happened, the community would lose another member or, in extremely bleak circumstances, sometimes multiple members would perish.

Then one year an Ojibwe hunter and his family got snowed in during a blizzard and were cut off from the rest of the community for the entire duration of an especially harsh winter. When the snow eventually melted and spring returned, the community came to the family's dwelling place and were horrified to discover the gnawed bones of the wife and children, but the hunter's bones were nowhere to be found. Soon a Wendigo was found lurking through the woods and the community finally knew the awful truth of what occurred. Thus the legend of the Wendigo was born. From that day forward the Ojibwe communities recounted the tale as a warning against the dangers of not preparing for winter and the fate of those that commit the ultimate taboo of cannibalism.

Osyka looked over the icy landscape, searching for a refuge from the storm and, hopefully, her pursuer. In the distance she could discern what appeared to be the mouth of a cave. It was her best bet at safety so she took off toward it. Behind her she could hear the Wendigo coming up out of the water. As she ran to the cave she prayed that it wasn't a dead end because she would have no choice but to confront the Wendigo if it followed her inside. It was a risk she had to take, though – staying out in this blizzard meant certain death.

Osyka shot through the cave opening at full speed; despite the blizzard outside, enough moonlight made it in so that she could see relatively well. Unfortunately, the cave wasn't very large, and she could see the light reflecting off the back wall as she neared it … There was nothing under her feet. She shot her arms out to the cave wall as she fell forward; the diameter of the hole wasn't very big but it appeared to be deep. With her legs and arms fully extended, she stopped herself from falling further.

Her heart pounded as she faced the darkness below. She kept her arms and one leg extended and kicked the other leg to the opposite side of the hole to span the gap. As she gained her footing she was able to upright herself by performing the splits with a foot on each side of the hole. Now she just needed to make her way back up to the top and climb out.

Easier said than done, she thought, but after a lot of sweat and effort she made it out.

As she sat on her knees in front of the hole and caught her breath she could hear the Wendigo clawing around and sniffing the air just outside the entrance of the cave. It was only a matter of minutes, possibly seconds, before it came in looking for her. She noticed an overhanging rock creating a lip over the inside mouth of the cave. If she could make it up in time before the Wendigo entered, she'd have a place to hide from it.

She scrambled up the rocky wall and lay down on her stomach at the overhang as she saw the Wendigo's head peek into the cave. Lying quietly above she was able to get a better look at it. She now saw it had long, dark hair that seemed oddly familiar. Something ahead darted back and forth then shot down into the hole, catching the creature's attention. It stood fully erect, its head nearly scraping the ceiling of the cave.

That thing must be at least ten feet tall.

It stepped further inside, curiously approaching the hole at the back of the cave. It leaned down to peer into it. Osyka knew this would be her only chance. She jumped down from the overhang and hit the ground running with her arms stretched out in front of her. The Wendigo turned to face her just as she shoved it into the hole. Before it disappeared below she saw one elongated arm reach out for her, a serpent tattoo coiled around the forearm … .

"KOI!" she screamed trying to grab his hand, but it was too late. She listened to him screeching, followed by a hard thud as he hit the bottom. It remained quiet for several seconds and she feared the worst, then she heard movement below and he started to wail and moan in pain. She felt bad but she'd only been defending herself.

She yelled down into the hole, "I'm sorry, Koi."

Osyka paced back and forth considering what to do next as a black fox crawled up from the hole. It was the shilombish, but this time when she looked into its eyes she saw something she had not seen before. The eyes that stared back at her now were the very same eyes that had watched her grow throughout the decade of her life so far, the same patient eyes that had watched her try and fail and urged her to try again despite it all. They were the eyes of her father.

"Dad? Is that you?" she asked, confused but hopeful.

The shilombish stared back at her and opened its mouth to speak for the first time. "It's me, Osyka."

It was the first time she'd heard her father's voice since before he passed away. The tears flowed fast and freely as she grabbed the fox and held him close. "Why didn't you tell me before?"

"I wanted to gain your trust first, Osyka, so you didn't think it was just some kind of elaborate trick. My actions would prove it to you, then hearing my voice would back my actions."

Osyka was a little upset that he hadn't made himself known to her sooner but it was perfectly in line with Nashoba's personality. Her father had always been very thoughtful and deliberate in his actions. "You're such a stubborn old man," she said laughing through her tears.

His voice choked a little as he said, "I knew you'd say that."

Koi's pitiful whimpering from below broke up their emotional reunion as they both stared down into the dim cavern below.

"Dad, how did he get that way? What happened that would make him give into the curse of the Wendigo? Koi knew the legend just like I did. Mom taught it to both of us growing up."

"That's why I'm here, Osyka. Your brother needs our

help," her father sighed, trying to find the right words. "As you get older, you'll learn that life doesn't always go as planned. When times get very hard and people grow desperate they'll do things in spite of what they believe in order to survive. After our plane crashed into that mountainside and we were stranded, he was put in a situation that no one should ever have to go through, and he made decisions he isn't proud of. In fact, those decisions tore apart the very fabric of his mind.

"A few of us survived that first night of despair, but by the second night we'd all either succumbed to our wounds or to the unrelenting cold, all except Koi." Nashoba was on the verge of sobbing as he continued. "He was on that God-forsaken rock for so many days, abandoned and all alone with no food and no one but the dead to keep him company. He lost himself up there, Osyka.

"By the time the rescuers found him, it was too late. There was so little of the old Koi left that he was unrecognizable as a man. They tried to help him, but he'd become something else entirely. Then they put him in that institution … ."

He hung his head in dismay and looked back up at her. "But you can save him, Osyka. You have all that is necessary in that bag. This entire journey has been leading up to this moment. Bring him back, remind him what it's like to be a man again. I believe in you."

Osyka stood there considering all that she'd learned. It was a lot to take in at once and now her brother's fate was left in her hands. She opened the bag and looked at the things she'd acquired. "Okay, let's do this."

She took off the deer hide and removed the hunting knife from the bag, using it to cut the hide into long strips. She tied the ends of the strips together to form a long, makeshift rope and drove the hunting knife into the ground in front of the hole, stomping the butt of it to drive it in up to the hilt. She then tied one end of her makeshift rope around the knife's handle and tossed the opposite end into the hole.

As she was doing this, Nashoba gathered a pile of sticks and rocks on the cave floor. "You're going to need to get a fire going if you expect to see anything down there," he said looking down into the hole. He was right. She spent some time getting a steady fire going, making sure there was enough light to where she was able to see the cavern's floor before climbing down.

When she reached the bottom she saw her brother had crawled into a corner and appeared to be nursing a broken leg. He was still a hideous sight to behold but now she had more pity than fear for him. His sunken eyes gazed up at her and he let loose a sorrowful cry, reminding Osyka of a scorned feline.

"Koi, it's all right. Everything's going to be all right. It's me your sister, Osyka. I'm going to help you. We're going to get you better, get you stronger, then we're going home. Together."

His malformed face stared back at her calmly but with a look of slight confusion. Her soothing tone and the compassion in her voice seemed strange to him. *It must seem like so long ago since someone spoke to him and showed him that they care,* she thought. The idea nearly broke her heart but she knew it was the truth. She needed to remind him of the brother he once was and that she knew was still buried somewhere deep inside him.

Nashoba crept up beside her, dropping a few sticks from his mouth at her feet. "You're going to need to make a splint for him so that it heals properly."

"How am I supposed to do that, Dad?"

"Don't worry, I'll walk you through it. These sticks should be enough to support his leg, but you'll need to take a couple of strips of hide from that rope you made to bind it."

It took patience and a lot of coaxing but Koi eventually allowed Osyka to approach him once he was sure that she meant him no harm. He didn't seem to acknowledge that she was his little sister and at one point when she was handling his leg a jolt of pain caused him to take a swipe at her, which she narrowly avoided, but he allowed her to splint his leg with Nashoba talking her through each step of the process. Osyka believed a certain degree of trust had been established between them.

Upon further inspection of the cavern Osyka discovered that the ground beneath them consisted more of soft dirt than stone. As she began breaking up a spot of earth she asked Nashoba if he thought enough light would make it inside during the day for her to grow something. He advised her to plant in a specific corner of the cavern floor that would be illuminated by the morning sun at the start of each day. She followed his instructions and planted several kernels of corn from her bag there.

She placed her bag on a rock slab and had Nashoba gather stones as she climbed up to the entrance of the cave and scooped up handfuls of snow. She used the rock slab as a table and used the stones to mash up the herbs she'd received from the three spirits. Mixing it with the snow, she created an herbal medicine concoction to help speed her brother's recovery process along and aid his body in fighting off the Wendigo sickness. She removed the last two corn cobs from her bag and slathered one of the cobs in the herbal medicine she'd made. She and Nashoba split the other cob between them.

When they finished Nashoba said, "It's probably going to be a little difficult to get him to eat that other cob. Even though corn is the natural food of his people, his body is still craving human flesh."

Osyka nodded her head. "Yeah, I figured. It's going to take some convincing to get him to do anything we want while he's like this, but we have to try."

Koi turned his head in disgust and pushed her away when she first put the corn to his mouth. She let him watch her take a bite of the cob so he understood it was food and that she wasn't trying to trick or poison him. After several more attempts he hesitantly took his first bite of it. He didn't appear to enjoy it but his swelling hunger finally forced him to give in and he ate the rest of the cob. Once he'd finished eating she stuffed his patch-covered denim jacket underneath his head as a pillow, while she and Nashoba curled up on the opposite side of the cavern to sleep.

Horrendous, high-pitched screams reverberated off the cavern walls. Osyka shot up to find her brother thrashing his limbs around as he lay face-up on the cave floor. He was drenched in cold sweat as if he was in the midst of a fever.

Nashoba had to yell in order for Osyka to hear him over Koi's screaming. "His body is fighting back. That's a good thing. You should give him more of your medicine."

She quickly threw some more of it together but she had no idea how to get it into his mouth with him flailing about like that. As if he'd read her mind Nashoba said, "You can give it to me. We foxes are known for our light feet. I'll drop it in his mouth and be back beside you before you can say Mississippi Magnolia."

She grabbed a small twig and put a thick glob of the herbal medicine at one end of it. Then she handed the twig to Nashoba who held the opposite end in his snout.

"Mississippi Ma—"

Before she'd finished Nashoba had darted on top of Koi, flung the medicine in his mouth, and was back sitting at her side.

She squinted at Nashoba. "Show-off!"

They shared a much-needed laugh before they turned their attention back to Koi. "His color seems to be returning, but we need to keep feeding him until the hunger of the Wendigo subsides."

She glanced at the spot where she'd planted the corn kernels and saw that the light of the morning sun was shining on the mound of soil from the cave entrance. A small green sprout was already peeking up from the dirt. By that evening, just as she'd hoped, there was a full-grown cornstalk that stood equal to her height. The three of them no longer had to ration the corn since this stalk, just as the previous, was self-renewing. They ate until they'd had their fill and Osyka continued coating Koi's corn with the herbal mixture she'd made.

This went on for several days. Nashoba would gather firewood in the mornings and Osyka would create a fire when it grew dark. She would make more of her medicine and Nashoba would help to administer it. She would prepare their dinner, then they would eat, sleep, then repeat. Soon Koi's fits subsided and he began to resemble the brother she'd always known. He was still frail and didn't talk much, but he cracked the occasional smile and acknowledged that they were a family.

Then one morning Nashoba woke Osyka and said, "I think it's time we start heading back. Your brother has the strength for the journey home now and I'm sure your mother and pokni are worried sick about you, but imagine how happy they'll be to have both you and Koi back home."

Osyka smiled at the thought. "And you too! Right, Dad?"

Nashoba turned without reply and lifted her bag with his nose until it slid down around his neck. "Come on, we better get going."

Osyka helped Koi to his feet and had him place his arm around her shoulders to help him walk with the busted leg. Nashoba climbed up out of the hole and Osyka and Koi followed using the rope of hide. Before they left the cave she took all the supplies she'd used and stuffed them in her bag for the journey back home. As they headed back out into the wilderness, Osyka was happily surprised to see that the sun had come out and was warming the landscape, melting much of the deep snow that had made her trek here so difficult.

Descending the rocky crag with Koi's injured leg proved to be an especially arduous task, but with patience the three of them reached the bottom. She knew they were nearing the base of the mountain when she saw the thick forests of spruce, then came the all-too-familiar drums. Osyka held her hand out, motioning for them to stop.

"Don't worry, I'll do the talking. Cheeby-aub-oozoo let me pass before, and I'm sure he will again. He's only guarding his domain." The large gray rabbit emerged from the forest, methodically examining each of them. He paused when he came to Nashoba. "Cheeby-aub-oozoo this is my father, Nashoba, and brother, Koi. We are simply passing through on the way home. We mean no harm – please let us pass."

Cheeby-aub-oozoo's gaze remained fixed on Nashoba.

This time Nashoba spoke. "Osyka, he wants me to go with him."

Osyka looked at Koi then back at Nashoba. "No, we finally have our family back together. I'm not going to just let him break us up again."

"Osyka, he and I made a deal. I had unfinished business in this world. I had to reunite you and your brother because I knew you could save him because you're both stronger together. But my being was always temporary and now my business here is done. I've got to move on to the next world where I belong."

Her eyes filled with tears as her face turned red with anger. "No! I won't let him do this! How can you say your business here is done when you still have a family? What about us? You're just going to abandon us and leave us to figure everything out on our own?"

Nashoba calmly lifted his head and looked into her eyes. "Don't you see, Osyka? You've already made it this far on your own. I tried to help you where I could but you never really needed me. I taught you and your brother all that I could in the time we had together and I'm amazed at how strong each of you are. You've both been put through things that no one should have to experience but my children are tough, you're both survivors. That's what I could teach you, but there's no way of getting around this or surviving it. It happens to us all; we just have to accept it. There's nothing I would love more than to stay with you, but I've already been given special treatment. More than so many others."

Osyka fell to her knees and cried. "I don't care how selfish it is, I want more time. You're my daddy and I want you to stay with me."

Nashoba quietly walked up to her and rubbed his

muzzle along the side of her face. She felt the fur of an animal against her cheek but smelled the scent of her father's cologne. "I know, baby, I know. Koi and I had time together to say goodbye on that mountaintop after the crash, but you and I, we never got the chance. This is it, please don't make me be the only one to say it. Don't make me be the bad guy."

Osyka was indignant in her silence as the tears ran down her face.

Nashoba sighed. "All right, if this is the way it's got to be …" He lifted his head and looked deep into her eyes. "Goodbye, my dear. I love you and I always will, you'll always be my little girl. Neither death nor time can ever change that. Take care of each other and be patient with your mother; she never intended on doing this alone. She's going to need both of you to be strong."

He looked up at Koi and Koi raised his hand to say bye, then Nashoba spent several moments looking into Osyka's eyes but she said nothing. He hung his head and turned to the large gray rabbit and together they began to walk toward the forest.

As they were about to cross over into the thick line of spruce trees Osyka said, "Goodbye, Dad."

Nashoba turned his head and looked back at her. A smile spread across the old fox's face as he and the rabbit crossed through the tree line and disappeared.

Koi and Osyka backtracked the way she had come without much difficulty this time. The animals and forest spirits they encountered acknowledged them with quiet reverence and let them pass without trouble. The siblings had endured their trials and, in turn, earned their respect. They crossed the river in her brother's canoe and soon she recognized the

woods she'd grown up around, the same woods she was forbidden of ever entering that stood beyond her grandmother's
house and where this long, strange journey had begun.

Then she saw the doorway, the iron arch with the wooden
bridge leading back into her grandmother's garden. The sun
was rising as they stood before it, preparing to cross over
the threshold and back into the world they'd known. Osyka
took a deep breath and looked at Koi. "Are you ready?"

He grinned and nodded his head.

"All right then, let's do this."

The bridge creaked and groaned as her feet shifted atop
the wooden planks and she found herself breaking into an
all-out run. As she left the garden and ran across the patch
of grass to the back porch she felt the morning dew soak her
feet. It was then that she realized she no longer had shoes
on, only her pajamas, and her buckskin bag of supplies was
missing. She stepped onto the porch and was about to open
the door when she stopped and looked around.

Where's Koi?

Her brother was nowhere to be found.

Osyka was reaching for the handle when the back door
swung wide open and her grandmother, Melinda, scooped her
up in her arms. "Where have you been, Osyka? I woke up and
you were gone. I was so terrified I called the sheriff's office and
they're sending a deputy out. Jesus Christ! Don't ever do something like that ever again. We've been worried sick about you."

Osyka stopped mid-hug and pulled her head away. "*We?*"

"Yes. We, Osyka," her mother said from the kitchen.

She looked over Melinda's shoulder and saw her mother
seated at the table with her grandmother from the opposite
side of the family, Namid. To Namid's right, sitting in his

favorite jacket with his lower leg propped up in a cast was her brother, Koi.

"Koi!" She screamed as she dropped from Melinda's arms and ran to him.

Koi held his arms open wide. "Heya, Squirt!"

They wrapped their arms around each other; he hugged her so tight that he lifted her feet off the ground.

She hugged him and kissed him on the cheek as she said, "I wasn't sure if I'd ever see you again."

He brought his head back and squinted at her in disbelief. "Yes, you were."

She looked at him with a perplexed expression on her face.

"You saved me, Osyka. I would've never survived up on that mountain without you."

Then he winked at her and kissed her on the forehead. Osyka was about to ask him what he meant, then she realized it didn't really matter. She buried her face into Koi's shoulder as tears of joy fell down her cheeks.

BLACK FLOWERS

Black flowers coming up through cracks in the sidewalk
Black flowers at your lover's grave
Black flowers blooming in the harlot's eyes
Black flowers on the anarchist's pin
Black flowers in the Devil's den

Black flowers upon your mistress's head
Black flowers for the tainted marriage bed
Black flowers at the center of each galaxy
Black flowers in the middle of a darkened forest
Black flowers sing the coming-of-age chorus

Black flowers in the end
Black flowers to begin again

CODA

Gene lifted the hood of his jacket over his head as the rain began to fall. He still had a long way to go before he made it home. As the rain grew heavier he decided to take refuge from the storm at a corner store – besides, he was getting thirsty from all the walking he'd done. The bell sounded as he stepped into the shop and walked to the back of the store to the refrigerated drinks. He'd heard people chatting when he first entered but now there was an uncomfortable silence and he had a feeling it was due to his presence. He could feel several eyes peering at his back; he tried to act normal as he picked up a bottle of soda.

The janitor that had been mopping took a few steps toward him with an obviously fake smile and made a point to look him directly in the face as he said, "Hey, how's it goin'?"

"I guess it's all right," Gene said as he turned and walked to the front counter.

He placed the soda on the counter and reached into his pocket for his wallet. When he looked up, the clerk was eyeing him nervously and standing perfectly still. Gene stood there with his wallet for several seconds before asking, "Are you gonna ring me up?"

The clerk reached for the drink, rang it up, and told him the price without ever taking his eyes off of him. Gene gave him the money, pocketed the change, grabbed his soda, and hurried out the door.

Jesus, what the fuck is everyone's problem in that place?

Thankfully the rain had lightened up some as he

continued his walk back home. After several minutes of angry confusion and trying to figure out what had just occurred, it hit him. He'd had his hood up the entire time he was in the convenience store. He laughed to himself. *God, I'm a dumbass! No wonder they were so nervous; they thought I was about to rob the place. I was starting to think I must be the first black dude they'd ever seen.*

A few minutes later he saw an Arish patrol car pass, it slowed for a moment then seemed to continue on its way only to then turn around a couple blocks further down. The lights flicked on and he knew what came next.

Shit, they seriously called the cops on me? He shook his head. Gene didn't have a rap sheet but he was aware of how tense interactions with the Arish police force could become, especially for a person of color. This was still the Deep South, after all.

A few months back they'd pulled his father over during a Sunday afternoon drive and even though Donald was nothing but respectful to the officers they insisted on doing a full search of the car. Gene remembered sitting on the curb growing angrier and angrier as each onlooker drove past, eyeing them as if they were already guilty of something. Of course, they found nothing, so they let Gene and his father leave but the ordeal left a lasting impression on him.

The police car pulled into the driveway of the nearest parking lot and a muscular, white police officer with a shaved head stepped out and walked over to him. "Hey, young man, where are you headed to?"

"I was just headed back home after taking a walk," said Gene.

"Really? Where do you live?"

Gene hesitated for a moment, not really wanting to tell

him but knowing it would look like he was hiding something if he didn't. "I live up the road on Charter Oak."

"Oh, okay. I know where that is. Do you have some ID on you?"

"Yes sir," Gene hoped the officer couldn't tell how nervous he was. "C-can I ask why you stopped me?"

"You seem a little tense. Is there something you need to tell me?"

He couldn't see the officer's eyes behind his sunglasses but he saw him shift his weight and gently rest a thumb on his holstered gun. *Shit, shit, shit!* He needed to calm down. His anxiety was only making things worse, and he didn't want to become another officer-involved shooting statistic. He needed to reset the situation. Gene took a deep breath and slowly exhaled. Then as calmly as possible he said, "No, sir. Can I know why you stopped me, though?"

The police officer stared at him for several seconds. "There's recently been some break-ins in this neighborhood and a couple of weeks ago someone robbed the gas station around the corner."

None of this looked very good for Gene, even though he was innocent, and he knew that. He carefully reached into his pocket for his wallet but as he removed it the billfold caught on the lip of his pants pocket and slipped from his hand. He quickly tried to grab it before it fell to the ground but the sudden movement alarmed the officer who whipped his gun out.

"Whoa, whoa, whoa! What the fuck is that?" screamed the officer as he raised the gun at Gene.

Gene froze with his hands open, looking down at his wallet on the ground. "It's my wallet. I dropped it. I was trying to get my ID out for you."

The police officer kept the gun pointed at him and said, "You stay still. I mean it – don't move! I'll get your wallet."

Gene stood perfectly still as his heart pounded inside his chest. "I'm not moving."

The officer leaned down and slipped Gene's wallet into his front shirt pocket, then told Gene to lift his hands and turn around. The officer started reading him his rights as he felt strong hands encircle his wrists and forcefully bring them behind his back and down to his waist. It was then that he realized he was being arrested. Cold metal cuffs slapped around his wrists, locking his hands behind him. Next thing he knew, he was being shoved down into the back of a police car.

Gene sat quietly on the wooden bench facing the front desk of the police department when he saw a woman in a hijab enter through the front doors. It was his mother, Tahara. He knew better than to expect his father since he was a barge worker that was often out of town but he'd still hoped for it, nonetheless. His father, Donald, would've understood the situation and sympathized with Gene, especially considering their last police encounter. His mother, on the other hand, was always quick to chastise him and sometimes she even went as far as to defend the opposing side when he got involved in confrontations.

Tahara walked up to Gene and asked him to explain everything that had happened leading up to him being brought in to the station. He recalled the events of the evening as best as he could, watching his mother's face grow more irritated with each passing second. When he finished she asked, "Is that all of it?"

He hung his head, ashamed of his own foolishness. "Yes ma'am."

He waited for the angry lecture that he knew was sure to follow. When it didn't come he looked up to see his mother standing at the front desk speaking with the clerk. She asked for the arresting officer's badge number then said, "I'd like to file a formal complaint."

Gene couldn't believe it.

Later, as his mother drove the two of them home, Gene looked over at her and said, "What made you decide to do that? I was sure you were about to chew me out. You never take my side."

"I know you think I'm hard on you, but it's for a reason. This world can be an unforgiving place, Gene, and I feel like it's my job to prepare you for it. If I'm too easy on you now it's only going to hurt you later when you're out on your own." Tahara sighed. "And I wish I could say in this day and age that this wasn't the case but the color of your skin isn't going to make it any easier for you. Instances like tonight show me that you're already learning that lesson.

"Now with that being said, don't you ever let anyone make you feel ashamed or guilty or treat you like a criminal because of that. I truly believe that's why the police officer arrested you tonight when he had no grounds to, but you did the right thing by not resisting or talking back to him there. You don't fight them there on the street because you'll lose every time – in fact, you might even lose your life. You fight them through the judicial system or even organize a protest if you must, that's the way you fight back and get to walk away with your life. Now it's not a perfect system, but it's the most likely method to keep you from getting shot."

Gene nodded his head as he stared out the window at the passing streetlights. His mother continued, "I'm also not telling you that every police officer is bad. They're just people, and some people are prejudiced so they carry that with them into their work. We can't forget where we live either. This is the South. We reside in the heartland of lynching and slavery; its lifeblood was cotton plantations that were run off the whipped, scarred backs of our people."

"I know all of this, Mom. I don't need a history lesson," he interjected.

"I'm sure you do know that, and I'm not trying to scare you but I need you to understand. There are plenty of good people here but many of them still carry the legacy of that past with them, whether they can admit it or not. Now this may be difficult for you to believe since we've worked in a partnership with so many of the Christian churches in the area, doing food drives and sheltering the homeless, but we've been in the community for a while at this point and built up a good reputation.

"It wasn't always that way, though – when we first tried to build the *masjid* here, the mayor and other prominent community leaders tried several times to stop construction. Then, when we did finally succeed in having it built, the day before we opened our doors someone vandalized it. They spray-painted, 'Go home, Arabs. We don't want terrorists here.' They were so ignorant and hateful they didn't even know we were a black-majority Muslim community, not that that would have necessarily made it better, but they probably didn't even realize such a thing existed."

He had to admit he was a little shocked. His mother was a well-known and respected member of the Arish Muslim community and she'd never told him about this incident.

It was silent for several seconds, then Gene placed his hand on hers and said, "Thanks, Mom."

She looked over at him and smiled. "You're welcome."

When they got home Gene was in a contemplative mood, he thought about race and his family's lineage as he looked at his mother's painting of famous black leaders throughout history as if they were all gathered in one time and place. There were the early leaders, such as Frederick Douglass and Harriet Tubman, all the way up to the modern-day figures of Nelson Mandela and President Barack Obama. He always felt a strong sense of responsibility when he looked at the eyes in the painting as if they were watching him and asking, "So what have you done lately?"

Gene sighed and walked toward the back of the house to his room. He glanced at the locked display case that held his grandfather's service rifle from the Vietnam War. It now belonged to his father, who'd promised it to Gene when he turned eighteen. Soon he'd take Gene to the shooting range to learn how to use it, just as his father had done with him decades before as a sort of familial rite of passage. He shook his head as he considered the sad irony of the fact that the grandson of a war vet could still be treated like a second-class citizen in the very country he'd served, but that was the truth of the matter.

He walked into his bedroom and collapsed face-first onto his bed. He didn't even bother undressing; it had been a long, exhausting night and sleep could not come soon enough.

Gene shot up out of bed when he felt the sun on his face; he knew he was running late if it was already that bright outside. He'd forgotten to set his alarm again, so he glanced at the clock on his bedside table. It read 6:51. He had nine minutes before the bus arrived. He normally would've taken a shower and changed his clothes but he didn't have time, so he brushed his teeth, sprayed on some cologne, and grabbed his backpack before rushing out the door.

The school bus was pulling up as he made it to the corner. He smiled. *Just in time.*

The doors opened and he climbed in and found an empty seat. He heard giggling in the seat in front of him and he knew the Ying Yang Twins were at it again. The Ying Yang Twins were two smart aleck sixth-graders named Jake and Darnell. They shared no actual similarities with the famous Atlanta rap duo; they'd simply earned the nickname on account that one of the boys was black and the other was white and they were always seen together.

Jake and Darnell peeked over the seat at him.

"Gene, we were wondering if you're still gonna be riding the school bus to work after you graduate?" said Darnell. He grinned wide, showing all of his teeth as more giggling flowed from the surrounding seats.

"Threw on my suit with my briefcase draggin', time to go hop on the cheese wagon," sang Jake as laughs erupted all around them.

Gene stared back at them unamused, "Shut up before I throw both your asses out that window."

This was followed by more laughter as the Ying Yang Twins quickly spun around, deciding not to test him. Gene shook his head, he wished he had a car or knew someone to give him a ride like some of the other seniors at school. Growing up in a lower-income area meant that he wasn't the only high school senior in his neighborhood that still rode the bus, but for some reason the other kids still liked to tease him about it anyway.

In first period, Gene stumbled through a Geometry test

he'd forgotten to study for. He went through the motions for most of his other classes until History class, his recent favorite. His History teacher, Mrs. Brooks, was having them watch the original *Roots* mini-series starring LeVar Burton. His initial interest in it was linked to being a science fiction fan and knowing that Burton had also portrayed the character of Lieutenant Commander Geordi La Forge in *Star Trek: The Next Generation*. As the mini-series progressed, he began to appreciate it on its own merits though; he felt a newfound respect for the hardships of his ancestors emerging as well as a curiosity for African culture.

The final class of the day was PE and he hated it. Many of the other guys enjoyed playing basketball and he did too, at first, until they got so competitive that it was no longer fun for him. The last time he'd played the final shot of the game was left to him and he missed it, causing his team to lose. Afterwards when he was showering in the locker room, his own teammates crowded around mocking him and calling him a "little bitch." When he returned to his locker he realized they'd stolen his clothes. That afternoon he was forced to ride the bus home in his sweaty gym shorts and tank top. After that incident he kept mostly to himself and only did the bare minimum that the PE coach required.

Recently, Gene had been gathering his nerve to ask out a pretty white girl in his English class named Alicia whom he'd been crushing on for a while. In an attempt to be discreet, he slipped a note into her hall locker and spent the rest of the day nervously awaiting a response. In gym that day she noticed him smiling at her from the opposite side of the bleachers as she sat with her girlfriends. A couple minutes later one of Alicia's friends walked over and handed him a note.

In the note, Alicia politely declined his offer to go to the movies with him. He was grateful that she at least let him down gently, though a few minutes later he heard the girls laughing at something Alicia was saying and they all looked his direction, immediately turning their heads when he made eye contact with them.

I should've figured, he thought, *it wasn't enough that she rejected me. Now they're all laughing at me, too.*

He decided to make the long walk home from school that afternoon. He needed to think and he wasn't in the mood to deal with the annoying middle-schoolers after the day he'd had. He'd made it about halfway home when he heard the *thump-thump* of gangsta rap approaching him. In his peripheral he saw a Caprice Classic on 22"s slowing down as it passed. He was on high-alert, ready to dive into the grass with his book bag as the passenger-side window rolled down.

He heard a familiar voice yell, "Yo, Babyface, what it do?" Gene hadn't heard that nickname in over a year so he knew it could only be one person. "It's your boy, Trigga."

Gene looked into the car and saw a dude with cornrows and prison tattoos mean-mugging him, then Keshawn leaned forward and flashed a smile with his gold grille. Keshawn and Gene had been friends his sophomore year before Keshawn dropped out. Keshawn liked using nicknames and often referred to himself in the third person as "Trigga" until it eventually caught on with others. He called Gene "Babyface" because he said he looked so young and innocent. Gene tried to make him stop until he realized it was pointless.

He stepped up to the passenger side window as Trigga said, "So how ya like my new whip?"

Gene eyed the car and then looked back at him before saying, "How'd you afford this?"

"Aw, you know, a little bit of this, a little bit of that. Adds up after a while you know."

Gene knew Trigga was one of the biggest dealers in the neighborhood. In fact, everyone in the neighborhood knew who each of the dealers were and who they worked for, but no one called the cops because it was too much of a risk to run your mouth if the wrong person found out. His parents told him to avoid those people and anyone associated with them. He remembered his father commenting that anyone could sell drugs, but a real man was responsible and got a legitimate job.

Trigga interrupted Gene's line of thought. "Babyface, this my man Giggles. He just got out the pen."

Gene locked eyes with him and they both nodded at each other.

Trigga continued, "You need a ride?"

Gene thought for a moment, he knew he should probably say no but he really didn't want to walk the rest of the way. Like a dumbass, he'd underestimated the humid heat of Arish in August. *Hell, what's one ride gonna hurt?*

"Yeah, I do."

Trigga smiled at him, "All right, bruh. Hop your ass in the backseat then."

Gene opened the door and threw his backpack in the back seat then climbed in. Trigga turned the gangsta rap back up as they pulled away from the curb. The bass shook the car as the subwoofers boomed through the seat. Trigga turned the music down for a second then glanced back at Gene, "Yo homie, you fuck with this?"

Gene sighed hoping he wasn't about to start an argument, "If you want me to be honest, nah, not really."

"Aw, you don't like rap, huh?"

"I didn't say that, you ever heard of the Universal Zulu Nation?"

Trigga looked at him a little confused. "Ain't that like a cult or something?"

Gene shook his head and chuckled. "It ain't a cult, fool. I was just gonna say did you know hip-hop started as a way to curb gang violence and unite people through break-dancing and music? No disrespect, but that G-shit is kind of a slap in the face to how it all started and what it represents if you ask me."

"Well, damn! Maybe I should start calling you 'Professor' instead since you're so smart, reading all those books and shit. Just remember before you get too uppity that while you're catching the bus home and sweating your ass off walking everywhere I'm riding on chrome." Trigga paused for a second, realizing he was sounding a bit defensive. Then he relaxed and said, "But enough with that shit. So for real who you into then?"

Gene shrugged. "I mean I like K-Dot and J. Cole."

Trigga nodded his head, causing his dreads to bob in front of his face. "Oh yeah, those 'woke' rappers. Always talking 'bout 'Fight for your rights' or some shit." He laughed.

Gene cracked a smile. "Yeah, something like that."

On the way home Trigga decided to stop by his house, leaving Gene and Giggles sitting in the car together as he ran inside. They sat in awkward silence for awhile as they waited for Trigga to return. Gene decided to break the ice first. "So how'd you get the name Giggles?"

He glared menacingly back at Gene. "First started calling me that after some shit that went down back in the pen."

"Like what?"

Giggles rubbed his chin. "Curious, ain't you?"

Gene shrugged. "Just making conversation."

"All right, Columbo." Giggles then shared a gruesomely detailed story of prison violence ending with the other inmates finding him laughing hysterically covered in another man's blood.

Gene shook his head and stifled an oncoming shiver. "Wish I hadn't asked."

Giggles grinned and turned his head back to the open car window as Trigga stepped out the front door of the house.

This fool is scary. What the hell is Keshawn hanging around him for?

Gene knew the answer though; it was all about appearances. Reputation by association. If he hung around tough guys no one would dare touch him, assuming he must be a tough guy as well. Almost immediately he had a second thought. *This guy's gotta be full of shit. If it was such common knowledge that he butchered someone in prison, there's no way he'd be out on the streets now.*

He hoped he was right but he couldn't be positive. Then Trigga leaned his head into the car. "Why don't you guys come in and chill for a bit? We'll watch some *Scarface* and blaze one. How 'bout it?"

Gene laughed. "*Scarface*? Haven't you already watched that movie like a billion times?"

"Man, shut up! Just come on, we haven't seen each other in like two years. We got some catching up to do."

Gene and Giggles got out of the car and followed him back inside. As they passed through the living room to the back of the house Gene saw a skinny, middle-aged woman lying on the couch in a dirty bathrobe, completely strung out. She started mumbling and saying Keshawn's name repeatedly but he ignored her as they followed him back to his room. He slammed the door behind Gene once they were inside.

Giggles looked at Trigga. "Who's the bitch on the couch?"

Trigga made a stern face and said, "That's my mom, mothafucka."

Giggles glanced at Gene and laughed, then turned back to Trigga. "Sorry."

Gene didn't find it funny, though.

Trigga shook his head and started rolling one up. He lit it, took a hit, and passed it to Giggles. "I'm gonna be outta here soon, anyway. Gonna get my own spot, some place nice. Just need a couple more racks and I'm up out this bitch." He grabbed the remote and turned on his flat screen, then hit another button and *Scarface* started playing.

This time Gene laughed as he took a hit off the blunt. "Had this shit cued up, ready to go, huh?"

Trigga laughed with him. "Man, this is like the only movie I own. It stays in the player. Hell, it's the only reason I bought one."

Gene smiled at Trigga and said, "You know that shit's outdated, right? I mean, do you own a VCR, too? You ever heard of something called Netflix?"

"Man, fuck you. 'Course I've heard of Netflix, but this is my favorite movie. I wanna own it, hold it in my hands. Bruh, I'm like the modern-day Tony Montana. I come out the gutter but I'mma end up on top of the world. His story is my story, but I'm smarter. I don't get high on my own supply," Trigga said proudly.

"Oh, really? He says with a fat-ass blunt in hand," Giggles said with a smirk.

Trigga squinted at him. "Psh! Please, you know I don't sell this shit no more. That's for the peons that just got in the biz. I moved on up into where the real money is now. Anyways," he said turning back to Gene, "as I was saying, if I can't hold it in my hands it ain't like it's really mine. Know what I'm saying?"

"Yeah, I feel ya. I guess you're just old school like my Pops. He's still listening to shit on wax, trying to tell me it sounds better with all those crackles and pops. He's all like, 'Boy, the blues is supposed to sound that way. Helps keep the feeling, gives it more soul.'" He laughed again. "Listening to all these old guys like Howlin' Wolf and Muddy Waters."

Trigga paused and stared at Gene with a puzzled expression on his face. "Okay, now you lost me. Who the hell is Muddy Waters? Sounds like some redneck shit." He took another puff and laughed.

Gene just shook his head as Trigga opened up a half-pint. Then he took a swig and passed it to Giggles. Giggles drank some then held it out to Gene but Gene shook his head.

"You don't want none?"

"He don't drink or eat pork, Giggles," said Trigga.

"Why not?"

"'Cause I don't want to," Gene responded.

Trigga interjected again, "His mom is one of the biggest Muslims in Arish."

Giggles stared back at him with a blank look. "So what?"

Trigga laughed. "Muslims don't drink or eat pork, fool."

"It's *haram*, or forbidden, in Islam," said Gene.

Giggles eyed Gene. "So you're a Muslim?"

"Man, I don't know what I am, but I think that religion's

got some good ideas. I respect it, I mean some of the smartest brothers I know that help elevate this community are Muslims. Muhammad Ali and Malcolm X were both Muslims," said Gene.

"So you'll blaze one but won't drink, huh?" said Giggles with a smirk.

"Man, how many times you heard about some fool trying to fight everybody at the club or wrapping their car around a tree after blazing one?" Gene paused waiting for Giggles to respond but he said nothing. "Now tell me how many times you heard about that after a mothafucka getting juiced?"

Giggles nodded his head in comprehension.

Gene sat back and took another puff off the blunt. "Exactly. Now get off my dick."

Trigga leaned back in his chair and laughed at the two of them. As it grew later Gene said he'd have to head home. Trigga told him he'd give him a ride and Gene accepted. As they pulled up in front of Gene's house, Trigga asked what time he went to school.

Gene crawled out of the backseat and looked back at him across Giggles from the passenger side window. "Man, it ain't been that long since you was out of school."

"All right, smart ass, so you gotta be there at 7:15?"

"Yeah."

"Well, I gotta get up early tomorrow anyways so I'll give you a ride. You shouldn't be riding the bus to school. You're like thirty-five or some shit now, right?"

Gene shot him a look, then said, "Man, fuck you … but I will take that ride." He laughed then shook his hand. "All right, see ya tomorrow morning then." He looked at Giggles preparing to shake his hand, but Giggles just sat looking forward so Gene turned around and walked to his front door. He checked the time on his phone and saw that he had several missed calls from his mom.

Shit, she's gonna be pissed at me.

He'd accidentally left his phone on silent mode after he'd left class. He carefully opened the door, praying that his mom was asleep so he wouldn't have to deal with her until morning. He stepped into the living room and saw her asleep on the couch with the television on. She'd unsuccessfully tried to wait up for him. He tiptoed down the hallway and opened his bedroom door when he heard Tahara say his name.

"Eugene?"

He sighed. He'd nearly made it, he walked back into the living room and said, "Yes, ma'am?"

She turned off the television and started in on him, "Where have you been? I was worried sick. I called you four times."

"I know, I just checked my phone when I got home and realized that I accidentally left it on silent. I was hanging out with some guys from school and lost track of the time."

"Who were you hanging out with?" she said.

"I just told you, some guys I know from school. I was friends with Keshawn my sophomore year and we hadn't hung out in a while. I just met the other guy, Giggles, tonight."

"Giggles? What kind of a name is that?"

"It's a nickname, Mom, not his actual name. Look, I'm sorry I didn't tell you where I was, but I'm really tired. Can I please just go to bed?"

She stood up from the couch and walked over to him and gave him a hug. "All right, I'll let you go to sleep, but remember to call me next— What is that smell on you? That better not be what I think it is, Eugene. I don't want you hanging around some reefer-smoking, no-good hood rats! You know we raised you better than that. You're not going to graduate and get into college if you're hanging around thugs, getting high all the time. You are forbidden to ever hang out with them again."

"Mom, chill out! It's just incense, Keshawn's mom has all these candles in her house."

"Boy, don't you lie to me! I know what incense smells like, and that is not incense. Look how bloodshot your eyes are!"

"That's 'cause I'm tired, Mom!"

She grabbed him by the shoulders and looked straight into his eyes. "I'm not joking, Eugene. Promise me you won't hang out with them again."

He didn't want to lie to his mother again but she wasn't giving him much of a choice. He sighed. "Okay, I promise I won't hang out with them anymore. Are you happy now?"

She smiled and hugged him, "Yes, I am, but you're grounded for a month."

"What! That's not fair, I just told you I wasn't going to— Ugh!"

He knew trying to argue his way out was useless, so he turned around and stormed back to his room, slamming the door behind him. He fell onto his bed but now he was too angry to sleep. He rolled over and glanced at his bookshelf for something to read. He removed a large book his father had come across in a used bookstore in one of the little port towns he stopped at while traveling up and down the river for his job.

It was an anthology of science fiction by black authors with some classic stories from two of his favorites, Octavia

Butler and Samuel Delany, as well as many others he was now becoming acquainted with. Gene sometimes imagined himself becoming a successful writer one day, but he figured it was probably just another pipe dream. He read until he could no longer hold his head up, then he turned out the light and drifted to sleep.

Gene sat up in bed. It was just before sunrise so his alarm had not gone off yet. He looked around the room; it was dim save for a few shadows caused by the streetlight outside. He got out of bed, took a shower, and started getting ready for class. A few minutes before seven he got a text from Trigga saying he was heading over. Gene told him to pick him up at the corner so his mom wouldn't see Trigga's car and she'd assume he took the bus as usual.

On the way to school Gene said, "So I appreciate the ride, but why the hell are you up this early? I definitely wouldn't be if I didn't have to."

"For me, one of the first casualties of the game was sleep. I barely sleep, and if I do it's with one eye on the door and one hand on my piece."

"Damn, that sounds rough. Why do you do that to yourself?" said Gene.

"I think it's funny that you act like I had a choice. You remember my grades, bruh. It's not like I was going to get a scholarship and my broke-ass mom sure ain't going to pay for college. Bitch don't even buy the groceries, I do." Trigga paused for a second and looked out the window. "To be honest, the main reason I offered you a ride was because we was friends from before and I know you a good dude. These days I don't feel like I got real friends, just people that hang around 'cause they want shit from me. Drugs, money, status. Nothin' but a bunch of fucking leeches."

Gene was surprised to find himself feeling sorry for Trigga rather than jealous. He was about to say something when they pulled into the front parking lot of the school.

"All right, Babyface, get your ass out my car and go hit them books!"

Gene laughed as he opened the door. "Shut up, fool. See you after?"

Trigga nodded his head. "Yeah I got you. See ya then."

As he climbed out of the Chevy Caprice and walked to the entrance of the high school he noticed several eyes watching him. He shrugged it off, tugged on his backpack and pushed through the front doors. The morning progressed normally at school but when he sat down at the lunch table with some classmates he could see a few people whispering and looking his direction from across the cafeteria.

"Damn, what's everyone's problem today? Everyone keeps looking at me whispering and shit."

His classmates looked at each other with knowing smirks on their faces. Then one kid named Terrance said, "Are you for real? You hopped out the car of the dude that deals to practically everybody in this school and you really didn't think people were gonna talk? You must be dumber than I thought."

Gene gave him a cold stare, then said, "Man, shut your ass up! I've known Keshawn since my sophomore year, we used to be pretty tight until he dropped out. I knew he dealt to some people here but I didn't know he was like *the guy* to go to 'round here."

Terrance laughed. "Yeah, I guess you wouldn't know that, Mr. Honor Roll Student. You're too busy with your nose in them books to keep up with who's who, but hey, that's cool. Maybe you can finally get laid now that everyone thinks you're a badass now." The other guys burst into laughter and Gene just shook his head.

At the end of the day Gene sat at the flagpole as each wave of students walked past. He heard Trigga approaching before he saw him thanks to the characteristic *thump-thump* of the deep bass emanating from his car as he came down the block. Gene sighed with disappointment when he saw Giggles sitting in the passenger seat as the car drove into the parking lot. He'd foolishly hoped that Giggles was just a one-time thing but, to Gene's dismay, it appeared Trigga and Giggles rolled together on a regular basis.

The car ascended the drive and parked in front of the flagpole. Several kids stopped and looked around at each other, nervously wondering what was about to happen, then Gene hopped up and crawled into the backseat. He smiled at the onlookers as they drove away. He had to admit it was nice to be noticed for a change, it seemed like he was finally getting the attention he deserved.

Gene leaned forward and said, "Hey man, no disrespect but I gotta get home early today. I got a lot of shit to do. That straight?"

Trigga side-eyed him and said, "You think I'm your personal fucking taxi service now or what?"

Gene sat forward. "Naw, man it ain't like that. I just can't get home late today, that's all."

Trigga laughed. "I'm just fucking with ya, but for real, we do have to make a quick stop on the way 'fore we drop you off. Giggles and I got some *bidness* to attend to and our man don't like us to be late."

Gene sighed and sat back in the seat. "All right."

Trigga pulled his car into the back alley behind a funeral home in an unfamiliar part of the city, then he and Giggles got out. Before closing the door Trigga turned to Gene. "Sorry, holmes, I gotta ask you to stay in the car. They don't take to new faces too well."

Gene glared back at him. "Then why'd you bring me here, fool? You coulda dropped me off."

"You think I didn't already think of that, mothafucka? I told you I ain't have the time. Chill out, listen to some music, we'll be back in a few."

He slammed the door as he and Giggles walked further into the alley and knocked on the iron outer door at the back of the funeral home. The inner door opened and a young guy looked them over suspiciously then started unlocking latches up and down the outer door before waving them inside. Gene leaned forward and turned off the radio then sat back in the seat and removed a book from his backpack. He glanced up from the book he was reading when a black SUV with tinted windows pulled to the curb and a good-looking black man in a business suit stepped out of the backseat and carefully surveyed his surroundings before entering the alley. Now the door was open and waiting for him to walk in, then it swiftly shut behind him.

The SUV at the curb stayed running as it waited for the man's return. As Gene watched, the passenger side window rolled down and a muscular man stared directly at him. Gene sunk down in the seat but it was too late. He knew the man had spotted him.

Shit, he thought, *I didn't sign up for this. I just wanted a ride home and now Trigga's gonna get my ass shot.*

In a moment of awful prescience he saw the barrel of a gun tap against the rear passenger side window. The muscular man yelled through the thin pane of glass, "Roll the mothafuckin' window down or I'mma light your ass up!"

Gene leaned over and rolled the window down.

"What are you doing out here, boy? You a snitch or something?"

Gene looked up at the man, trying to hide his fear but knowing it must be obvious on his face. "No sir, I'm just waiting on my friend Keshawn to come out. He told me to wait in the car for him. He's giving me a ride home; that's it, I swear."

The man eyed him for several seconds then said, "All right, we'll see about that."

Ten awkwardly long minutes later the businessman came out through the iron door and glanced at the two of them. "What's going on, Darryl?"

"I caught this boy spying and asked him exactly what he was doing out here," said the muscular man.

The businessman glared at Gene and walked over to the car. "Is that true, young man?"

Gene's eyes widened in panic as he shook his head. "No sir, I wasn't spying. I'm waiting for Keshawn, he's giving me a ride home, that's all. He said he had a meeting he couldn't be late for and that I should wait for him out in the car."

As Gene finished, Trigga, Giggles, and several other young men came out of the door and into the alley. The businessman glanced at Trigga. "Keshawn, is this young man with you?"

"Aw, yeah that's my boy, Babyface. He's cool, don't worry 'bout him."

The businessman eyed Trigga with a look of disbelief then said, "Come here, Keshawn. I need a word with you."

Gene couldn't make out most of what was being said since they were speaking in hushed voices until Trigga suddenly burst forth, " … But I thought if he just stayed in the car … ."

Darryl stepped over and placed a hand on Trigga's shoulder giving him a stern glance; this caused him to lower his voice once more. A minute later he was nodding his head in agreement, then he and Giggles headed back to the car. They got into the front seats and after the doors were shut Gene said, "Knew it was a bad idea."

"Shut up or I'll make your ass walk home," said Trigga as he started the car up.

Gene watched Darryl and the businessman climb back into the black SUV before it pulled off and disappeared down the street. The other young men that had exited the funeral home with Trigga and Giggles left in various cars or headed off down the sidewalk back out into the city.

When they pulled up in front of Gene's home he thanked Trigga for the ride and hopped out before sprinting inside the house. He was lucky for a change, his mom hadn't made it home yet so he was still in the clear. He went back to his room and started on his homework, and when his mom arrived he acted as if nothing ever happened. The remainder of the evening passed uneventfully and he was thankful for a decent night's sleep.

Despite everything that happened the day before, Gene accepted a ride from Trigga once again, hoping that the events of the previous day would not be the norm. In class Gene could tell his rep was growing; more people talked to him that morning than ever before. It amazed him how fast word spread about who he associated with and how much of a difference it made in the way people viewed him. In English class he noticed Alicia look back and smile at him, followed by a few of her friends later on. He figured they still thought he was a joke.

During PE Gene sat on the bleachers watching the other guys play basketball until the coach forced him to play as well. As soon as he made a shot he pulled out and got back to the bleachers. He'd been sitting for a few minutes when White Mike came up and sat beside him.

"I was never that into b-ball neither, man," said White Mike.

Gene laughed. "I liked it until I realized everyone started taking it so seriously. I thought it was supposed to be a game played for fun. It ain't like there's talent scouts watching us or something."

White Mike nodded his head. "I know what you saying, bruh."

Gene had spoken to him a couple times before but never more than a few words, and mostly only when Gene had initiated it. White Mike was probably the most well-known white boy in Cedar Ridge High School. Trigga was the guy you went to for street drugs, but White Mike was the hook-up for prescription meds, which he facilitated through his after-school job as a pharmacy tech.

"So you 'bout to ask if I need some Xannies or something?" Gene said with a grin.

"Shit, man, lower your voice." He leaned in and spoke in a hushed tone. "I gotta keep that on the DL for real, some of these kids 'round here are straight snitches. They got no respect for the game. Actually I just figured I'd let you know that girl Alicia over there wants on your dick bad, dude. She keeps talking 'bout you and if I was you I'd hit that. She's one of the hottest bitches in class, ya ask me."

"Are you serious? I asked her out like two days ago and she said no. Now you're saying she's into me?"

White Mike held his hands up, "Hey man, I'm just telling you what I heard her saying. I guess she had a change a heart or something. Who knows with these high school girls? They're crazy."

Gene sat back and looked across the gym to where Alicia was sitting with her friends. She made eye contact with him for a split-second then sheepishly looked away. He could see it now. He shook his head. "Well, I guess I know her game now. She's nothing but a status chaser."

White Mike gave him a confused look.

"As in, I got a little respect now and she suddenly thinks I'm good enough for her when I wasn't a couple days ago."

White Mike shook his head. "Damn, that's cold. Well, look at it this way, you might still get a li'l head out of it."

Gene burst into laughter and hit him in the shoulder. "You're wrong for that!"

White Mike leaned back in and lowered his voice. "Well, since I did you a favor telling you 'bout Alicia, you think you could do me one in return?"

Here it comes, Gene thought, *the real reason he came over to talk to me.*

"I know you tight with Trigga and all and you know what my supply is and what his supply is. I wanted to see if you could check if he was interested in doing a li'l business deal, if you know what I'm saying? I won't get into the details right now, but we would both benefit from it."

"Man, to tell you the truth I'm not involved in that stuff with him. I mean, I know he's into it and all but that's his own business," said Gene.

"Yeah, but you two's homies, right? You could at least tell him, let him know about my proposition," said White Mike.

Gene gave up. "Sure, I guess so, but no promises."

"Hell yeah, no pressure." He stood up and grabbed Gene's hand and gave him a pat on the shoulder. "We straight."

"See ya, Mike."

He was about to turn and walk away but stopped. "To be honest, my name ain't even Mike, it's Stephen. People just started calling me White Mike 'cause they thought it was funny and it rhymed."

"Seriously?"

"For real, just thought you should know."

"All right then, later Stephen." Gene sat there smiling and shaking his head. He paused for a moment then stood and started walking across to the other side of the gym. He knew it was petty but he was going to make Alicia regret being so shallow.

He smiled as he approached the group of girls and a few returned the smile. "Hey, Alicia!"

Alicia stopped mid-sentence and turned his way. "Yes, Gene?" she said with a smirk as if she knew what he was about to ask.

"You busy Friday night?" he said as he propped his foot on the bottom bleacher attempting to exude an air of confidence he didn't truly possess.

"Maybe, who wants to know?"

"I do. You wanna catch a movie Friday night? It's on me. You give me your number and I'll pick you up at seven."

Alicia smiled and looked at the girls sitting around her but there was no reaction. They were all awaiting her response. She opened her purse, took out a piece of paper, and scribbled her number onto it. Then she had one of her friends pass it down to him. "Text me and I'll give you my address so you can come pick me up."

Gene glanced at the piece of paper then stuffed it into his pocket. "Aight, cool."

He casually strolled away as her friends resumed the frantic chatter they'd put on hold when he first approached. He grinned to himself as he imagined Alicia dolling herself up on Friday night with nervous expectation awaiting his arrival that would never come. He knew it was wrong but he didn't care. A girl like her deserved to be knocked down off her pedestal every once in a while.

Gene was pleasantly surprised when Trigga picked him up after school minus Giggles that afternoon, but he was uncharacteristically pensive allowing several minutes to pass without music or conversation until Gene broke the ice.

"Are you okay, man? You seem … *different* today."

Trigga paused. "Do you believe in God? Like somebody that's looking out for you and that's got special plans and shit for your life?"

"Yeah, I do. Don't you?"

"I used to, but these days it's really starting to seem like some fairy tale shit that people say to ignore what's right in their face." Trigga spoke to the windshield, never turning to make eye contact.

"Right in their face? What you mean?" said Gene.

"Like everyone's ignoring the truth. We're all just walking around down here trying to figure this shit out and hustling to stay alive, but there ain't no one looking out for us. We're on our own in this life. Shit don't mean shit and then you die. That's what these streets taught me, there ain't no God looking out for us. I saw this one dude blow another kid's brains out right in front of me and Jesus or Allah didn't step in and stop that shit. That's when I started carrying a strap, man. Make sure that don't ever happen to me."

Gene sat quietly trying to figure out what brought this change on. "Did something happen to Giggles? Is that why he's not here? Why you're saying all this, acting like this?"

"Naw, man, Giggles is straight. I just don't want to be around him all the time. He's always acting so mothafuckin' hard, can't even have a real conversation with him like I can with you, Babyface." Trigga finally looked over at Gene and smiled for the first time. "That's why you're my boy. He's just someone I keep around for protection."

Gene nodded his head, he thought for a moment, then spoke slowly choosing his words carefully. "Bruh, you ever thought about getting like a *legit* job?"

Trigga shot an angry look back at him. "What the fuck you trying to say? Like I don't work for my money?"

"No disrespect intended. I mean like a job where you pay taxes, clock in, clock out, something 9 to 5. Something outside the streets. I mean, I know you won't make near as much but you also won't have to carry a piece on you. You might be able to start getting sleep again. Just saying, real talk, that might be worth the pay cut."

Trigga laughed and shook his head skeptically. "We might be the same age but you talk like a kid in kindergarten, like you got a lotta learning to do."

This time it was Gene who looked upset.

Trigga continued, "You think I didn't try to get a 'legit-imate' job? Man, those pasty assholes in their offices take one look at my name: Keshawn. They don't even give me a chance. That name's as bad as having a rap sheet with a couple bodies on it. I guess maybe if I changed my name to Brett or Cody I'd be all right, though."

Gene shrugged his shoulders. "I don't know what to tell you. I just know these streets ain't a long-term answer. They chew fools up and spit 'em out like it ain't nothing. How many old-timers you know still slangin'?"

Trigga thought for a moment then nodded his head, "Aight, keeping it one hunnid. I feel ya, it is a young man's game. You gotta keep on moving like a shark 'cause the moment you stop some scary bastard is gonna roll up and take a bite out ya and fill your spot."

As he finished they pulled up in front of Gene's house. His mom's car wasn't in the driveway so he was still in the clear. Gene leaned over and thanked him for the ride, as he climbed out of the car Trigga called after him.

"So I know your mom's all on your ass like the Feds at the moment but Giggles and I are gonna hit up the club on Saturday night, maybe hunt for some shorties. Any chance you wanna roll with us?"

He paused and thought for a moment, he was pretty sure his mom had a fundraising engagement with the mosque Saturday that would keep her out late. He believed he could pull it off without getting caught if he didn't stay out too long. He nodded at Trigga, "Yeah, let's do it." Gene turned and was about to walk away. "Just make sure Giggles keeps it under control, okay?"

Trigga laughed. "No prob, man. Catch your ass on the flipside!" Then he sped off down the street.

Gene grinned, shaking his head as he opened his front door.

Gene rode shotgun on the way to Club Absinthe and Giggles sat in the backseat for a change. They all laughed as Gene joked about standing up Alicia the night before. "Damn, that boy is so fine. I guess I'll give him another hour," he said in a mock-feminine voice impersonating her.

"You shoulda fucked her first then dumped her ass," said Giggles. "That woulda really been payback. That's how I woulda played it."

Trigga nodded. "Yeah, but Babyface here didn't want to lose his V-card to a girl he's not in love with, right?"

Giggles erupted with laughter. "Yo, for real, you still a virgin, dawg?"

"Hell no, I ain't a virgin!" Gene lied straight to their faces.

Trigga looked at Gene skeptically as Giggles responded, "I was about to say, at your age I already smashed like five or six bitches, bruh."

"Speaking of, I need to get some cut up tonight or I'mma go crazy," said Trigga.

Giggles nodded, "I'm right there with ya."

"So how the fuck are we supposed to get inside? Ain't Club Absinthe one of those twenty-one and up places?" said Gene.

"Don't worry, I got the hook-up. I mean, Giggles don't gotta worry 'cause he's an old man. But I know the guy running the door tonight so he'll let us in, no questions asked," responded Trigga.

When they arrived the bouncer gave Trigga a nod and Trigga covertly slapped some cash in his hand and the man let them in without being frisked or ID'ed. As they entered the crowded club Trigga turned back to Gene and grinned then yelled over the music, "See, I told you I got you, dawg!"

Gene smiled and nodded his head as he scanned the scenery.

"Aight boys, y'all have fun, I'm 'bout to get turnt up!" Trigga threw his hands in the air as he wandered off to the bar.

Giggles disappeared into the crowded dance floor without saying a word and Gene found himself standing alone feeling a little awkward and self-conscious but he attempted to play it off like he was cool with it. Luckily the place was so full that he was able to lose himself in the herd of people. He liked the look of the place with the neon lights, mirrored ceiling, and chrome barstools. He pushed through the dance floor toward an empty booth he'd spotted on the other side of the club.

As Gene took a seat in the booth he had to admit to himself that Trigga had picked a good spot for gorgeous women; it seemed everywhere he looked there was another pretty girl. He burst into laughter when he spotted Giggles grinding against a curvy, light-skinned woman in a short dress. Not that Gene wasn't envious of him, but it was still funny to see a stone-faced guy like him trying to bump 'n' grind.

Trigga hopped into the booth across from Gene with a glass in hand. "Sure ya don't want something to drink, man? I got you."

Gene could tell Trigga was already starting to feel the alcohol but he wasn't quite drunk. "Nah, I'm good. I think you've had enough for the both of us."

Trigga laughed. "Psssh, I'm just getting started."

The two of them sat at the booth silently for several minutes as Trigga bobbed his head, vibing with the music. Gene still wasn't quite gelling with the place; he was on edge tonight for some reason and he didn't believe it was just a side effect of his sobriety. When his attention returned to Trigga he was eyeing a pretty woman in a revealing top and skin-tight jeans sitting at the bar.

Trigga stood from the table, smiled at Gene and said, "Wish me luck!" before wandering back to the bar.

Gene shook his head and looked back to the dance floor. Giggles was dancing with the same lady from before and whispering into her ear when a shocked expression spread across her face and she spun around and slapped him. Gene fought the urge to laugh as she marched off the dance floor, leaving Giggles embarrassed with a group of stunned onlookers. Giggles locked eyes with Gene and headed over to his table as Gene tried to pretend like he'd seen nothing.

"Fuck this place! These bitches are all uptight and shit! Find Trigga and tell him we should go to the Palazzo instead. It's two blocks over on Sunset Ave," Giggles yelled over the music.

Gene nodded his head, he was happy to get out of this place. He figured he'd let them drop him off at the bus stop and they could head on to the Palazzo on their own. As he made his way over to the bar he exchanged glances with a uniquely attractive white woman in a floral dress drinking a cosmo. He gave her a friendly smile, which she returned as he passed.

Gene leaned over Trigga's shoulder. "Giggles wants to get out of here. He said there's a better place two blocks down called the Palazzo."

Trigga spun around on the stool and Gene noticed he slurred a little as he said, "What? There aren't enough women here for him or something? Or he just doesn't have any game?"

Gene laughed. "Man, I don't know. He just wanted me to tell you."

Trigga glanced back over at the woman he'd come to the bar for, there was now a guy sitting next to her chatting her up. "Damn, dude! You just cock-blocked me and that bastard swooped right in!"

Gene gave him an apologetic look.

Trigga sighed and shook his head. "Aight, let's get outta here."

When Trigga got up from the stool he stumbled a bit and Gene caught him. "You sure you're okay to drive, man?"

Trigga looked offended. "Hell yeah, I'm good. I just slipped, somebody musta spilled their drink there."

Gene kept an eye on Trigga's driving as the Caprice eased out of the parking lot and onto the street. They stopped at a red light and Gene leaned forward to ask about a ride to the bus stop when a beat-up Suburban pulled alongside them.

Giggles tapped Trigga's arm and said, "You won't believe who just pulled up next to us."

Trigga glanced out the passenger side window. "Holy shit!"

Gene didn't recognize the young man puffing on a cigarette in the Suburban.

"Can you believe that mothafucka would dare show his face in this city after making that hit on the bossman's nephew last year? He's got to be fucking crazy!" Giggles was whispering even though the tinted windows were rolled up. "If we put his punk ass down, we'll be set for life. Boss'll make sure of that, no doubt."

Trigga removed the semi-automatic pistol from the waistband of his pants and paused for a moment.

Gene grabbed the door latch and Giggles hit the child

safety locks trapping him in the back of the car. "No way, let me the fuck out of this car! I don't want nothing to do with this."

Giggles spun around and looked him dead in the eyes, "You lie down in that seat and shut your fucking mouth or I swear I'll do you right after we finish him."

Gene had never considered himself a coward but he realized in this moment he had no option but to back down. He slumped into the back seat and started praying.

Trigga lifted the gun and took aim as Giggles leaned the seat back and rolled down the passenger window. The man in the Suburban was oblivious as he sat at the intersection staring up at the red light.

"C'mon, bruh, once that light turns green you missed your chance," whispered Giggles.

Trigga's gun hand started to tremble, the traffic light flashed green, and Gene heard the Suburban's engine rev as it began to pull away.

"You want people to call you Trigga like you a gunman, but you're just a little bitch. Gimme that!" Giggles snatched the gun from Trigga's hand as he squeezed off several shots into the Suburban's driver's side door. The truck fish-tailed, nearly careening into a light pole, then with a squeal of tires it took off down the street and made its getaway.

"I'm done with this shit! My mom was right, you two are nothin' but a couple of hood rats!" Gene yelled as he reached forward and hit the child's lock switch, then jumped out of the back of the car.

He took off running without looking back. He heard Trigga's tires spin out as the car sped down the street. Onlookers began to pour out of nearby bars and restaurants as he ran past. He heard someone report a shooting in front of Club Absinthe on their phone. He jumped a fence into an abandoned lot and hid in some tall grass. Several minutes later he heard a police siren.

Gene took out his phone to check the time as he neared his neighborhood. It was late and he was screwed, no doubt about that. He'd either left his wallet in the club or, God forbid, Trigga's backseat, leaving him with no bus fare. So he was forced to walk all the way home. He knew his mom was going to be home waiting up for him ready to chew his ass out the moment he stepped through the door, especially since he was already grounded from leaving the house to begin with.

Gene was okay with that, though; tonight had been the final wake-up call he'd needed. No matter how bad his mom got on his case he knew that she loved him and was only looking out for him. He could survive losing all his privileges and a few months of grounding, but if he kept hanging around Trigga and Giggles he literally might not survive at all. Either that or he could end up serving a prison sentence for being an accomplice to some more dumb shit they pulled. For all he knew that might happen anyway if any bystanders were able to connect him to the shooting.

As he turned the corner to the street he lived on a police car sped past with its lights and sirens blaring. He watched as it skid to a stop in front of his house and two officers hopped out with guns drawn. He broke into an all-out run. As he neared his front yard he saw Trigga's Chevy Caprice parked behind his mom's Honda in the driveway. There was a body slumped over in the passenger seat of Trigga's car. He saw the cornrows and immediately knew it was Giggles.

"I live here. Man, what the fuck is going on?" he screamed.

The two police officers turned to him, the black officer responded first, "Sir, I'm going to need you to calm down. The neighbor reported multiple shots fired and that someone made a forced entry into this home. Can you tell us anything?"

Gene saw the neighbors across the street peering out the window. He glanced back to Giggles's lifeless body in the car. "That's this dude named Keshawn's car and that's his friend, Giggles. I don't know why he got shot." Gene looked to his house. The door frame was broken with a few bullet holes around the lock and the front door was slightly ajar. The curtains were closed but he could tell the living room lights were on. "I think he's in there with my mom, but I don't—"

"Gene!" He heard his mom cry out, then it was cut short by another voice inside.

"Shut up, bitch!" There was no uncertainty left, it was Trigga.

"Baby, know I love you. No matter what happens!"

Gene heard a slap, followed by, "I told you to shut up."

The black officer looked at his Latina partner and said, "I'm radioing for backup."

Gene studied the two police officers as the one put in a call for a hostage situation. He didn't feel right standing there and doing nothing while his own mother was in danger, especially when he was responsible for putting her there to begin with. It also didn't help that he had no faith in the Arish police department. They'd shown their true colors time and time again when dealing with his family. The message seemed to be clear: they were not to be trusted.

Gene had one last look at them. "Nah, fuck this!" He took off toward the chain-link fence that surrounded his backyard.

The Latina officer ran after him, "Sir, stop. We've got it under control. You're only going to make the situation worse."

He hopped over the fence into his backyard and immediately started prying open his parents' bedroom window at the opposite end of the house. Luckily, he'd done it a couple times before when he'd forgotten his keys and hadn't had the patience to wait for his mom to get home. Gene climbed across the window sill into the bedroom. He then eased their door open and peered down the hallway. Trigga was still facing toward the front door with a gun to Tahara's head, crying, and passionately cursing at both Gene and the Arish police department. He was entirely unaware of Gene's presence in the house.

He snuck along the hallway staying low and quiet, hoping Trigga would keep his attention focused outside. Gene could smell the booze wafting off of him; he'd never seen someone so unhinged. The look in his eyes reminded Gene of a cornered animal lashing out in defense. Then those wild, desperate eyes found him.

Trigga spun around still clutching Gene's mom, holding her in front of him as a shield. "Thought you were gonna sneak up on me and knife me in the back or something, huh, Babyface?"

There was no use in trying to hide any longer so Gene stood up and confronted him. "What the hell's gotten into you, man? Why're you doing this, and why'd you kill Giggles?"

Trigga seethed as he spoke. "I had to listen to that mothafucka go on and on 'bout how I'm a pussy and a paper gangsta, then I get home and my fucking mom's dead. She OD'ed, finally put too much of that shit in her veins. That was it for me, the final cherry on top of the shit-sundae that is my life. So I walked back outside, got in the car, and put a bullet in his face. Showed him how gangsta I could be ... He ain't laughing no more.

"You always thought you were so much better than me, you were just slumming with the gutter boy when we hung out. Trying to act like you on some street shit."

Gene interrupted, "Man, what are you talking about? We grew up in the same neighborhood."

"Psh, as if that matters. You got everything: a mom and dad who love you, good grades, bright future. I mean, how could you not succeed? But that don't mean you're better than me, you just got better circumstances. I bet you probably think God is just shining His light down on you, right? But there ain't no God watching over you, protecting you. You just been lucky, until now that is. We're all on our own down here and I'm 'bout to prove it to you. I'm gonna take something dear to you and bring you down to my level. Then everyone can see how great you really are!"

"Come on, man. She didn't do nothing to anyone," Gene pleaded. "She's a good person, one of the few there are left. Please don't hurt her, if you have to hurt someone, hurt me. I'm the one you're mad at."

Tahara burst forth, "No, don't hurt my baby. Not Gene, he—"

Trigga smacked her in the head with the butt of the gun. "Didn't I tell you to shut the fuck up?"

An angry sneer spread over Gene's face.

Trigga laughed at him. "There ya go, that's how it starts. You starting to learn how the world really is." The expression on his face suddenly changed as he looked past Gene. "You really brought a cop up in here, mothafucka?!"

Trigga yanked the gun away from Tahara's head and fired several rounds off to Gene's left. He took advantage of the momentary distraction and leapt forward, pulling her from Trigga's grasp as he and his mother fell to the floor. Almost without thinking he spun around to face Trigga while using his body to shield her. In his peripheral he watched the Latina police officer collapse against the wall. Then slowly slide away, leaving a trail of blood back into the hallway, where she slumped to the floor.

Gene felt disgusted as the guilt hit him. She'd followed him inside. He could hear the frantic voices of her fellow officers repeatedly asking for her status through the radio with no response.

I brushed her off and that woman just gave her life for my family, he thought.

Trigga turned to Gene and Tahara as they lay on the floor looking up at him. He pointed the gun at both of them. "Get out of the way, Gene!"

Gene shook his head, "Man, you know I'm not going to do that."

"Then I'll just shoot you and shoot her afterwards anyway."

"I guess that's how it's gotta be then," said Gene, "but if you think I'm just gonna move out of the way and *let* you hurt my momma, then you're crazy."

Tahara pleaded with Gene to get off her so Trigga wouldn't hurt him as well, but Gene wouldn't allow it.

"Aight, have it your way." Trigga lifted the gun and brought his finger to the trigger.

Gene closed his eyes and there was a loud pop as blood sprayed over his face. He opened his eyes to see Trigga's surprised expression as he cupped a hand over the blood steadily pouring from his abdomen. He stumbled toward the kitchen and fell. Gene's father stood at the end of the hallway, holding the service rifle his own father had used in Vietnam.

"Donald!" his mother screamed with relief.

She and Gene stood up and ran to his father as the family embraced one another. Gene heard something move as his father's strong hands shoved him and his mother back behind him and aimed the service rifle once again. Trigga had rolled onto his back and was beginning to lift the gun when Donald spoke, "Young man, I don't want to kill you but if you point that gun at my family again …."

Trigga stared coldly back at them. "You should go ahead and kill me; I'm as good as dead now."

Donald's voice softened and Gene recognized the compassion that his father was known for. "There's always time enough to change."

Trigga managed a pained laugh as he glanced at Gene. "Now I see where that foolish optimism comes from …" Trigga returned his eyes to Gene's father now. "You really thought I planned on walking out of this?"

Trigga brought the gun to his head as Gene threw his hands up to stop him but the bullet had already left the chamber. Gene's family looked away from the gruesome scene.

Tahara stared at Donald with amazement. "I don't understand. When did you get here?"

His father kissed her and said, "I had a coworker give me a ride home earlier. Then I fell asleep; I didn't even hear you get home. I woke up when that boy started kicking and shooting the front door down. I was able to get Pop's rifle out of the display case in the hallway without him spotting me, though. I loaded it in the bathroom and was waiting for the right moment when Gene snuck in."

Gene shook his head. "I didn't even notice Grandpa's rifle was missing."

His father pointed to the female officer lying in the hallway. "See how she's holding up. She was still breathing but unconscious when I checked on her. Make her a tourniquet with our bath towels. I'm going to try to get help. They still have no idea what's going on in here."

Gene grabbed some towels and went to the wounded officer as his father slowly eased open the front door with his hands raised above his head. Gene glanced at her name tag. "Officer Rivera, can you hear me? We're going to try to get you some help." Gene was shocked when the woman's eyes flickered open. "Oh my god, you're okay."

Officer Rivera winced. "I wouldn't go that far, but I'm still kicking." Gene wrapped a towel around her wounded shoulder as she used her other hand to press a towel firmly against her leg, plugging another wound. He noticed another bullet hole at her chest but the slug was still lodged in her Kevlar vest, which had saved her life.

Gene could hear the police captain giving his father instructions through the megaphone when gunfire erupted once again.

"Cop killer!"

His father fell back through the doorway and landed on the carpet. Tahara screamed as Gene looked on in horror at his father on the living room floor.

"Goddamnit, hold your fire!" Barked the captain through the megaphone.

His father rolled clear of the doorway and frantically patted himself down expecting to find blood on his hands.

When he realized he hadn't been hit he looked up at Tahara and Gene. "It's okay, I'm all right."

"Jesus Christ," said Officer Rivera in disbelief. "Okay. Tensions are pretty high at the moment and they're angry … They know one of their own's been shot and they never got an ID on the shooter … I need to radio out to them, let them know what happened. That I'm still alive. Then if you guys can help me, we'll walk out together."

Gene and his mother helped Officer Rivera sit up and she radioed to the captain that the perpetrator was dead and only unarmed bystanders remained. She then added against the captain's orders that the family was now going to escort her outside. Gene and his father each put an arm underneath Officer Rivera's shoulders and helped her to her feet. Then his mother followed behind them with her hands raised as they stepped outside to a mass of police cars and ambulances.

Gene sat in the back of an ambulance as a paramedic checked him out and Gene repeatedly told him he was okay. Once the medic cleared him, he stepped out of the ambulance to find his parents waiting. He smiled at both of them and hugged them once again. His father informed them that they would need to head to the station for more questioning as well as find another place to stay for the night since their home was currently a crime scene.

As they rode up to the station together, Gene's young mind wandered. He thought of the mistreatment of his people by the Arish police department and the inherent racism of the city in which he lived. He thought of how Keshawn was chewed up and spit out by the streets and the entire system that profited from them. He thought of the young female police officer and the bullet she took for his family. He thought of the wisdom and love passed onto him from both of his parents.

Gene stared out the window as the streetlights passed above his head and dared himself to hope. *Maybe, just maybe, everything will be all right in the long run.*

About the Author

Jesse Muchmore grew up in northern Mississippi with the bustling city of Memphis only a few minutes away over the state line. At a young age he had hopes of starting a punk band, but soon realized he did not possess even the rudimentary talents required to do that. Despite three decades of living in the Bible Belt, the traditional, conservative values never really sat well with him, but he later found his tribe within the works of Flannery O'Connor, William Faulkner, and Cormac McCarthy. This eventually culminated in a writing degree from the University of Memphis. These days those influences have merged with the strange ambience of Lovecraft, the quirky pessimism of Vonnegut, and the forward-thinking of Philip K. Dick to create something altogether unique.

He now lives in Florida with his wife and two cats.

www.jessemuchmore.com

60998502R00140

Made in the USA
Columbia, SC
20 June 2019